**the raz/shumaker prairie schooner
book prize in fiction**

editor
kwame dawes

thanks for this riot
stories

janelle bassett

university of nebraska press • lincoln

Acknowledgments for the use of previously published material appear
on page 171, which constitutes an extension of the copyright page.

The University of Nebraska Press is part of a land-grant institution with campuses
and programs on the past, present, and future homelands of the Pawnee, Ponca,
Otoe-Missouria, Omaha, Dakota, Lakota, Kaw, Cheyenne, and Arapaho Peoples,
as well as those of the relocated Ho-Chunk, Sac and Fox, and Iowa Peoples.

Library of Congress Cataloging-in-Publication Data
Names: Bassett, Janelle, author.
Title: Thanks for this riot: stories / Janelle Bassett.
Other titles: Thanks for this riot (Compilation)
Description: Lincoln: University of Nebraska Press, 2024. | Series:
The Raz/Shumaker Prairie Schooner book prize in fiction
Identifiers: LCCN 2023057870
ISBN 9781496240330 (paperback)
ISBN 9781496240736 (epub)
ISBN 9781496240743 (pdf)
Subjects: BISAC: FICTION / Short Stories (single author) |
FICTION / Feminist | LCGFT: Short stories.
Classification: LCC PS3602.A8478 T47 2024 |
DDC 813/.6—dc23/eng/20240212
LC record available at https://lccn.loc.gov/2023057870

Designed and set in Minion Pro by K. Andresen.

For Colin,
who once asked me
to write down
what I was thinking

Joy, said Grandma, is resistance. Oh, I said.
To what? Then she was off laughing again
and there was nothing anybody could do about it.
—Miriam Toews, *Fright Night*

contents

thanks for this riot

External

Riots

Threats and Violence

More Restrictive Than Supportive

When I wore a strapless bra for the first time, my mom told me I was a sinner because God made breasts to be lifted from above like ascending angels. I'd gotten a spaghetti-strap tank top at the mall, using the money I made selling my porcelain dolls at our yard sale. I was trading in my dainty girlhood to become a grown lady whose shoulders needed public attention. It was time—my hips had expanded to the point that I could no longer fit in my hiding place between the side of the sofa and the base of the staircase.

But all the bras I owned undermined the debut I craved for my shoulders. They covered the skin I wanted to show, while letting everyone know I still wore sports bras, even though I'd been kicked off the softball team for spitting a loogie into the little yellow coin purse my coach took with her to the laundromat. I had no choice about that loogie. Coach laughed along after Wendy B. said I looked like a wobbly bar stool when I was at bat, instead of letting Wendy know that wasn't a very nice way to talk.

There wasn't enough yard sale money left over to buy myself a strapless. I got only $25 for my dollies. I should have gotten much more—there were twelve dolls in my collection, and each one was in pristine condition. I never took them up trees, struck matches on their cheeks, or bit off their fingertips the way I wanted to. I respected them as a collection. I dusted them on Sundays. But the first woman who came to our yard sale offered $25—even though I had them marked at $115—and Mom told me it was a sin to haggle, especially with my elders, who'd been alive long enough to know about the true worth of certain objects. So I had to watch this person wearing a Tasmanian Devil T-shirt wrap all my dolls up in the deflated kiddie pool my mother had the gall to throw in for free, while knowing that she was walking away with damn near $100 of my mall money.

Grandma Cleo took pity on me and my shoulders and gave me the strapless bra she had worn to her prom. (Grandma Cleo spoke to an easier, friendlier God than the one my parents consulted. The congregation held hands in the pews at her church across town. Grandma's God could take a joke, where my parents' God demanded to know what, exactly, was so funny.) The bra was stiff and lacy—more restrictive than supportive—and it smelled like a musty, colorless yearbook. But the bra didn't show a bit under my tank top, so I would wear it out.

"Can I go out?" I asked my mom, three days before my strapless bra debut.

"What? When? With whom?"

I knew there would be a lot of questions. Other than school, I'd never gone anywhere without my parents. Mom had attended all my softball practices, sitting in the bleachers under her sun hat, yelling, "Look alive, ladies! It's important to stay in 'ready position' even when the ball is heading the opposite direction." And Mom's elbow touched mine all through the Westgood Mall—dressing rooms and check-outs were no exception. She even double-checked the math on my receipts. And when our family went to the fabric store to buy supplies for the preemie quilts Mom donated to the children's hospital, I wasn't allowed to peruse the yarn or the beads in further aisles. *You're just the kind of girl a kidnapper would love to take away forever.* I didn't ask what qualities I had that made me that kind of girl, or why my parents petted my hair so lovingly after they said it, like being highly kidnappable was a trait they admired about me and made them especially proud to call their own.

I had never before asked my parents to go out because I knew their answer would be, "We *would* let you go to the movies, but the thing is that we really want to see your face again, so the answer is no." There was no good retort to that logic, other than knocking the merits of my own face—pointing out the asymmetry, the weak chin, the avalanche cheekbones. But ever since I got too big to wedge myself into my hiding spot—a spot that never failed to help me feel right and simple, like a complacent stack of meat and bones—I'd gotten a new sharp edge about me, and I wanted to cut my parents with it. Along with sunshine on my shoulders, I craved discord.

But my mother quickly warmed to the idea of an outing. Apparently, she'd been preparing for the moment when I would assert my right to separate and had only been waiting for me to ask. She laid out two options for activities I was allowed to do, unsupervised, with my school friends. She said wholesome teens could go bowling (but *not* form leagues) or they could ride paddle boats (but *only* in calm, still water—boating over waves was too provocative).

Both options had the potential to thrill me. I'd done nothing, I wasn't hard to thrill. My wildest private daydream was to walk down the aisle of fake flowers at Joann Fabrics, alone, imagining that the plastic flowers were catcalling me while demeaning me passive-aggressively, like those golden afternoon blooms from *Alice in Wonderland*. I would have *loved* the chance to bowl or paddle without my mother there to point out who, exactly, would kidnap me if given the opportunity. (Once, in a miniatures museum, she accused the man transfixed by the teeny three-story log cabin inhabited by clothed possums of being "the 'napper among us." I recognized this man as my bus driver—a person who could easily take me and my backpack home with him on any given day.) Yet I balked at my mother's pre-approved activity options, calling them "lazy" and "sinful," words that made very little sense when applied to our conversation but were nevertheless the most condemning adjectives in her vocabulary.

"Plus we already decided on go-karts," I told her, which was the first time I said the word "we" to my mother instead of *about* my mother. *I now have a context outside of your reach, old miss.*

Mom looked like she wanted to pull my hair or shove my face into a holy text, but she only nodded while maintaining a level of eye contact that made my burgeoning sharp edges gleam.

"I don't know how I feel about go-karting, Lydia. Do you happen to know the shape of the track? Is it one big oval? I'd feel more comfortable knowing you'd be making sharp turns every so often, so the vibrations and curves won't lull you into forgetting your morals."

I saw a wobble in her eyes; my challenges were causing my mother to lose a small percentage of her certainty. "Do your own research," I told her as I headed toward the mirror in my room. I was eager to see if my haughty tone had brought out any new symmetry in my face. "Pull up an aerial map and take a look."

* * *

On tank top go-kart day, Mom made her quip about the angels who wanted to hold my titties, but otherwise she let me out the door without making dire threats or clipping a long leash onto my belt loop. But before I hopped into Andrea's mother's car, she called out, "If you find yourself locked in a trunk, remember to kick out a brake light and wiggle your fingers out the hole to alert other cars that you're being held against your will, possibly across state lines."

Andrea was wearing a tube top, so right away I was outranked and outshined. But still, I said, "Hey, thanks for the ride, you look so cute, your car is so clean," which were too many things to say at once. Feeling outdone made me babble. When we pulled up to Randi's house, I was pleased to see her exit wearing an oversized T-shirt. I'd try to stand next to her once we were in public, so I'd look hot and free by comparison.

Andrea, Randi, and I were not really close as friends. We hadn't been BFFs since elementary. We didn't share clothes or have inside jokes. What happened was that our gym teacher paired up judo matches based on weight, and the three of us, being the same size, ended up spending a lot of time in each other's armpits and ponytails. Plus, we'd all been denied entry into the upper echelon of girls—the ones who walked around with their foreheads facing forward instead of down—which forged an understanding, if not a camaraderie.

* * *

I let my mother believe Andrea's mom would stay at the track with us the whole time, even though Andrea had told me all about the drop-off plan. But once I was being dropped off, I felt unsure. Also a little naked. Did I have enough money? Who would point me toward the bathroom? Would Randi and Andrea talk to me as we waited in line, or would I have to stand silently, trying to look as happy about the top half of my outfit as I had hoped to be? Was the sun brighter than normal? Were Randi's teeth sharper than before? Did that lady just growl? As Andrea's mother drove away, I wanted to hop in her trunk for safety. I'd be a good passenger, kicking nothing, giving all her music choices an approving thumbs up from my safe spot in the dark.

* * *

The building Randi, Andrea, and I entered smelled sweet, almost like pixie sticks, plus there were body smells (sweat, breath, pee) mixed with the scent of hot plastic and warm plugs—machines at work. The chaos came from all the smelly bodies—in lines, in circles, weaving and leaving—and from flashing lights, electronic sound effects (ding-ing, ka-powing, a bass beat), and layer upon layer of human sounds (laughter, chatter, "Hey, Jason").

Randi looked like a person capable of processing all the movement and smells around her. "Let's do the laser tag maze first."

"Then the rock wall." Andrea was placidly watching a child attempt to pry the purse from his mother's shoulder.

I pulled my bra back into place while trying to make it look like I was only giving myself a small, encouraging hug. "I . . . thought this was a go-kart place."

"This is an entertainment complex."

"Yeah, it's called Mondo Amusements. Go-karts aren't mondo on their own."

7

Andrea and Randi walked ahead while they said the things I should have already known. I quickly followed, so that I didn't get swirled away into a group of friends who liked me even less, who'd never been flat in the gymnasium with a mouthful of my hair.

"I only brought ten dollars," I told them. "I can't afford to do all this other stuff."

We walked by signs that said GEM MINING // FOAM FIGHTS with an arrow pointing left and ESCAPE ROOM // FLAME VORTEX with a right-facing arrow. I was relieved that my friends didn't turn and hoped the activities straight ahead were more like PILLOW DEN or STATIONARY CIRCLE.

"Oh my god, Lydia, haven't you been here before?"

"Didn't you look at the website?"

No, I hadn't. I wasn't allowed to use the computer without Mother at my elbow, nodding or shaking about where I wanted to point my cursor. Didn't *she* check this place out before giving me permission—at least ensuring the sharp turns she wanted to keep me on the straight and narrow? I felt certain that my mom would have revoked her permission if she knew about the rock wall. *"And then they've got you right where they want you, Lydia—fifteen feet off the ground and tied up with the rope of their choosing."*

We stopped at the entrance for the laser tag maze. The sign told us laser tag cost $8.99 and was a "great team building exercise!" Randi and Andrea paid using their phones, and I dug my single ten-dollar bill out of my pocket. My friends' money was faceless and untouchable, and mine harbored germs and long-dead eyebrows.

I said, "I can only afford to do one thing," and put my shameful currency back in my pocket. I was ready to tell them I avoided *all* mazes after the skinned knees I'd earned doing a three-legged race with my mother through a hay bale maze set up in a church parking lot—but Randi and Andrea were already making their way into the small room ahead of us, joining a group of people circling around a woman in green shorts giving safety instructions. The woman stood in front of a wall rack of black laser guns, all aimed at the floor. "The first rule of the laser tag maze is to have b-i-g mondo fun! The second rule is to keep both feet on the floor at all times: no climbing, no skipping, no hopping. Now, raise your hand if you've had aneurysms or a recent surgery."

"There's an observation deck." The man my friends paid to enter was pointing to a railing high above the maze I was trying to avoid. "You could help your little pals, warn them what's around the corner."

I didn't like this man pointing and suggesting where I should put my body. It was my mother's fault, I knew, that I suspected him of setting up some sort of trap for me in the observation deck, that I worried I'd never return to my set life course if I climbed up there to tell my friends to make two rights and then a left toward freedom.

"No thanks." I backed away and made a quick turn around the corner, toward the foam fights. I stood against the wall and pulled my grandma's strapless back up over my breasts. Once I felt reasonably sure the laser man was no longer looking at me, I slipped into the midst of a large, loud family. The parents and three children were all talking at once, recapping the putt-putt experience they just shared. The only family member who seemed to be doing any listening was the preverbal baby strapped to the father's chest. I maneuvered closer to the baby, who smiled at me—perhaps because I wasn't making it try to comprehend any of my words.

I stayed with the family until we reached the familiar territory of the entrance area. I found a bench and decided the room's commotion was easier to handle sitting down. I wished I had enough money for a snack. I smelled meat and cheese and maybe waffle cones. My mother should have considered that, without proper energy, I'd never be able to outrun a man with a lasso or a huge net.

Only groups of people walked by. No one was alone. No one was stationary. No one had goosebumps down their arms where their sleeves should be. The longer I sat watching people trade their money for twenty-minute thrills, the madder I got at my mother for allowing me to sit there, and then the madder I got at *myself* for voluntarily putting my life back underneath my mother's control while I was experiencing my very first freedom.

A woman walked by pushing a double stroller. Perhaps those twin toddlers were heading to the batting cages. When the woman was just past me, she stopped pushing to wade through her purse. She pulled out a package of tissues and used one to dab at her side-by-side offspring.

"Excuse me?" I felt 80 percent sure a woman with two young children would not have the energy to kidnap a scraggly, asymmetrical thirteen-year-old. "May I have a tissue?"

She handed me a tissue without curiosity or sympathy, probably assuming I was old enough to be sitting alone anywhere. Even on a pier. Even in an alley. Even in a mall dressing room with three to five tank tops, or near the base of a man-made rock wall surrounded by the swirl of entertainment commerce. I thanked her and she nodded before pushing her babies toward the game room. Perhaps those twin toddlers were going to expertly dance-dance along with a video game screen.

I pulled apart the tissue layers and put the two thin pieces over my shoulders. For warmth. For protection. To replace my friends, to form a new group. I wondered how much longer Randi and Andrea would be navigating the laser maze. I wondered, too, if they'd even bother to look for me before moving on to the next activity, which I couldn't afford anyway. *Doubtful,* my tissues and I agreed.

Eventually I stood up, just to prove to myself I still had some control over the situation. When my shoulder tissues fell to the ground, I left them there.

I scanned my surroundings for someone non-threatening. *Nope, he has mirrored sunglasses on top of his head. Secretive. Deceptive. Wolf-like. Not her, she's over thirty and wearing a belted dress. She's probably jealous enough of my enviable youth to belt me to a bike rack and leave me there, hoping my pert skin will become weather-beaten. No, no, no, no—a row of children who look like they know how to skateboard. They could team up and wheel me off.*

The next person who walked by was wearing a shirt my mother owned—a brown button-up blouse with black flowers. The silky shirt really needed another color, a yellow or white to brighten the drab. But still, a known shirt. I moved closer.

"Uhm, do you know where the go-karts are?"

The woman in my mother's shirt stopped and turned her whole body toward mine. She came close. "Are you okay, honey? You look upset. Do you need help?" She put her warm hand on my upper arm, calming the goosebumps there. "Would you like to use my phone? Let me walk you to the . . ."

I seized up, closed my eyes, put my hands over my ears. I wanted simple directions, not to shove myself underneath the crushing force of a mother's concern. I shrugged her hand off and ran past her, farther from the entrance area. I heard her calling out directions to the go-kart track, but I pressed my hands harder into my ears—creating suction—until all I could hear was my pulse and the creak of my own force. Eyes closed, ears pressed, I understood everything: My mother didn't really care if I was dragged into the woods, weak and hungry. She really didn't care if a kidnapper held me captive in a small wooden box. She was only genuinely concerned about my soul, but my body was the part of me she could boss around. She hyped up the world's danger in order to control me, used fear as a weapon against the lure of ungodly influences and against the forward momentum I was born with.

I squeezed past a group in neon green "Mason Family Reunion: It's Every Mason for Themselves!" T-shirts to find the door to the outdoor activities. I pushed the door open with my side, then took my hands off my ears.

I could hear go-kart motors in the distance. All I had to do was move toward the noise without being struck by a putt-putt ball or getting myself stuck inside a batting cage. Easy, surely. I felt the sun on my shoulders and regained some sense of purpose. I was out. My bra was not showing. My mother was elsewhere. My dolls were sold off. Not one person was luring me into their van. The go-karts were right there, straight ahead.

The teenager with the "Billie J" name tag said, "That's $8.99 for you, but passengers are free." I held my arms out and spun myself around, a gesture I hoped conveyed the same *I got nothin'* as turning your pockets inside out. "Just me." Billie J took my ten-dollar bill and handed me a few coins.

"Aren't there helmets?" I asked.

She mocked my spinning gesture—*do you see helmets?*—so I went past her and got in line for the course. The line moved quickly, meaning I'd just paid $8.99-plus-tax for one of the briefest thrills Mondo had to offer. Two slices of pizza would have thrilled me for *at least* seven minutes.

Riders rushed by, enjoying their short stints, while the girl behind me asked to cut in front of me in line. "It's pretty much an emergency."

"How so?" She was small, maybe six, easy to look down on, easy to demand explanations from.

"My mom said she's pulling out of the parking lot in ten minutes, with or without me." She was wearing a purple jumper while hopping up and down. Instead of bending down to her level to whisper that she had been dealt a bad, irresponsible mother, I decided to pretend she no longer existed.

When I turned back, a boy my age was stepping out of a go-kart, leaving it empty for the next person in line, which—while I'd been denying the eager request of a small child—had become me. The motor was still running, so I lowered myself down into the kart's dark-colored humming and put my hands on the wheel. I wished I had thought to paint my fingernails. Gripping black foam with red nails would have made me feel all the more out-of-the-house.

I wasn't sure how hard to push the gas pedal—I'd never even ridden our lawn mower. I wanted to get used to the feeling of sitting in the machine before engaging any gears. *This humming is the baseline.*

"Just go!" The little girl had stopped hopping to rush me. Hellion. I stomped the pedal but looked straight ahead so I could pretend it had been my own idea to get going. The go-kart jolted forward, but I kept control and took the first turn easily. Once I got going, the speed was not a threat but a realignment. My body could finally keep pace with my mind. No lag, no push and pull—I was a unified being cutting through the wind.

The course was all curves. From above, the track must have looked like a splat, or an amoeba. The sensation of going as fast as I wanted was even better than my wildest daydream—though I did (as an inside joke) imagine a chorus of artificial flowers, their stems twisted around and through the chain-link fence, singing, "Look at you go, you lousy hussy." Taking the final turn of my first lap, I noticed that I could feel wind on my stomach. When I looked down, my bra (and the top of the breasts it was struggling to contain) was fully visible. The speed had blown the loose neck and thin straps of my tank top down until it was even with my armpits. I yanked my top back up, thankful that no other rider was close enough to get a real eyeful.

Right then I passed the line of people waiting. The girl was gone. I ran through the possible reasons for her absence—a turn of her own, a mom, a 'napper—but since my top had been blown back down, I was more focused on staying decent. I sat up straight and pulled my shoulders back to become a wider mannequin for my shirt, hoping that if the fabric were pulled taught, there'd be less flapping and flashing. That strategy didn't help, so I pulled the neck of the shirt up and held it in place with my chin. This caused my stomach to poke out the bottom, so I ended up outshining Andrea and her tube top after all.

I slowed down a bit, since it was harder to keep my eyes on the track while craning to use my chin like a chip-clip. I still enjoyed my ride, even reigned in and bent over. The turns felt predictable. I had grown used to the wind. Other riders passed me, but I don't think they meant anything by it. On the section of the track closest to the building, I scanned the milling crowd for a purple jumper. No sign.

In the foreground, the flowers I'd imagined in the fence had been replaced by real hands, as a row of onlookers watched the go-kart action with their fingers poked through the fence. Soon I was passing them, only feet away, and a man with hairy fingers was looking right at me and laughing at the sight of me and my shirt problem. Laughing meanly. Mockingly. As a threat. It was hard to get a good look at him, but from what I could tell he looked exactly like a person I hated.

I sped back up, gaining speed and resentment with each turn. I hated the little girl for making me worried enough to look anywhere other than the road ahead. Turn. I hated the drivers I was easily passing. Turn. I hated my friends for leaving me alone and for having parents who took them to Mondo on a semi-regular basis. Turn. I hated my mother for not letting me out before that day and also for letting me out that day. Turn. I hated those twins who still got to be pushed around by their mommy. Turn.

Then it all felt too irreparably bad—the angry turns but also the tone of the past six months. Before then, I had never understood the word "fuming." Before then, I hadn't spat into any coin purses. I was sweet, more or less. I was kind, here and there. I had positive interactions. I decided how I felt, wasn't so reactive. I trusted people. Was part of becoming a woman learning to be on high alert for when you've been wronged and then diligently keeping a tally? Or was this new capacity for pure hate the last gasp of my little girl self, like a final tantrum? I resented both thoughts, and the craning made my neck hurt like hell.

I'd done a full lap of fuming by then, and I was close to passing the man at the fence again. My ride would be over soon, so I lifted my chin and let the wind do what it wanted with my clothing. Fly, bra. Fly, shoulders. The exposure became a choice as I decided I would ram right into the fence instead of going on by—scaring him, stopping him, showing him—and I didn't waste any time debating whether that kind of premeditated crashing was the act of a thoughtless girl or a vengeful woman. I simply gave myself full permission.

The Crowded Private Cottage

Grandpa and I have fallen into a routine: wake, denounce the day, share a memory, eat a bread product, dress with difficulty, say something cheery yet false, state an intention, eat an animal product, fail to share a memory, pretend to want to go outside, open mail, touch hands, mention Grandma, move objects from table to counter, console ourselves by consoling each other, have a small but presentable dinner, then make slower movements and use gentler tones, slower and slower, gentler and gentler, until lights out.

I've been staying with my eighty-year-old grandfather for six months, without breaks or thanks. They say old people might be able to get vaccinated by the end of the year, but I find it hard to believe anything good or hopeful will happen from here on out. At the beginning of the pandemic in March, Mom panicked and yanked him out of the care facility she had recently placed him in. Luckily, we hadn't yet sold his house and luckily, I—having forgotten to embark on a real career—had a pretty open schedule.

This routine with Grandpa has been diminishing my spirit and wasting my youth, but as soon as my brother comes to temporarily relieve me of my caretaking duties—as soon as I get in the car to drive to my rented cottage—I wonder if, maybe, Grandpa wants to come with me. We could play checkers in a different room, and I could comb his hair and tell him he looks like Cary Grant again. He smiled the first time.

I booked my Airbnb based on the fact that it was close to the highway but not *on* the highway. I wanted a break from the hustle-bustle, but I still wanted to be able to hear, faintly, what it was up to. The space also had a "sleeping nook" and "luxurious tablecloths," which appealed to me because my goals for my week away were to sleep in a folded position and eat off a material much finer than my clothing.

Once I'm off the highway, I roll my windows down and let the wind remind me that I'm still young, that the pace at which I've been living wasn't meant for me. When I pull up to the "private cottage," a person wearing a short billowy dress under a fur coat is chasing a small child while reminding the child that she has to wear her jellies if she wants to spend time in the wooded area!

A different person, with a mustache, calls from a lounge chair to leave the child alone, she's having a necessary tactile experience, she'll feel more grounded after having her soles on the earth, probably take better naps, wait and see.

The little family infesting my private weekend appears to be totally oblivious and relatively relaxed. *Oh shit*, I think. *Rich people.*

* * *

It turns out my cottage is actually a duplex, my living space only half of what I thought. It turns out the people staying in the other half are celebrities. (The adults, I mean—the child has yet to prove herself.) The phrase they actually used during our brief, fumbly, and distanced introduction was: "We're in comedy." I nodded and said oh cool, but the phrase sticks with me. As I unpack my clothes and wonder whether Grandpa is having toast or a bagel today and as I wipe down the door knobs and faucet handles so they don't make me sick—possibly very sick—and when I see that my second cousin is spreading the idea that the virus is a punishment from God for letting women rent U-hauls and I see, also, that his profile picture is a doctored image of the bad president lifting weights, I think, *We're in comedy. Surely we are.*

My side of the duplex has recently been redecorated by a moose enthusiast. The pictures from the Airbnb listing showed a themeless decor that wasn't at all the color of bean dip. The browns and tans on the walls and furniture make me feel like dirt. Low. And oh look, the paper towel holder has antlers.

I unfold the yellow skirt I so recently unpacked and drape it on the back of the couch, a sunspot amid the mud. I hear the comedy couple through the wall—not their exact words but tones and cadences suggesting that what they're saying is funny. Dah-dah-DAH-dah-dah-dah-dah, like a sardonic Christmas carol.

I wonder how the walls would translate the conversations I have with Grandpa. I try to keep talking the whole time I give him a bath, asking him questions about his childhood (his mother's favorite card game, the color of his bike, the number of stitches from the fall into the manhole) so that he's too busy casting back to feel embarrassed by his nudity or the fact that his age has made bathing an ordeal instead of a delight. He likes being interviewed, being seen as a source, even a naked and frail one. "Now let me see," he'll say as I add more hot water so he doesn't get the shivers. Maybe, through the wall, it sounds like mum-pum-mum-pum when he says his mother played a type of solitaire but never taught him how to play.

Instead of surrendering to the calming effects of nature and solitude the way I had imagined—flat, pantsless, unneeded, and even-breathed—I'm beginning my relaxing weekend hunched over on the couch, relentlessly googling the jokers on the other side of the wall. It's easy to find their names and their film and TV credits and their most viral posts and to pay money to stream their stand-up specials.

I grab my laptop and fish my headphones out of my purse—I don't want my duplex-mates to know I'm in training to become their biggest fan. I'll start with her special—*Jena Gregory's BAD LUCK DIME STORE KINK HERO*—because she's the more successful of the two, according to the size of their Instagram followings, though most of the comments on her photos are men congratulating themselves on the fact that they find her fuckable even though she's over thirty-five and has a lot to say.

Jena starts her set with a bit about how breastfeeding made her breasts hard and sleek, like a set of dolphins arcing through ocean waves. After she finished nursing, she would set up small obstacles, like cubes of cheese or a deck of cards, for her "sea pig tits" to jump over. She demonstrates the chest leap with the microphone, making a splashing sound but keeping her shirt on.

This is all more amusing than funny, but a lot of the humor is in the way she tells it. She has a sleepy voice and body, barely upright all-in-all, possibly held from behind by one of those waist-cinching stands for expensive dolls. Her stage persona is in her lack of stage presence. The joke is that she is mostly elsewhere.

I stop the show every couple minutes to check my phone, making sure there are no messages from my brother Neil that say bad fall or new cough or too late.

Jena goes in hard on the way parenthood has impacted her career more than her husband's. *"He can come and go like the McRib, but when I want to leave the house, I have to write four pages of handwritten instructions and kick my leg until the hysterical child comes off."*

This doesn't make me laugh, but I think *sure* and scratch my inner thigh with my heel. I go back and forth between the two screens for half an hour, between Jena's jokes about being needed and the confirmations that I'm *not* urgently needed. Laptop, phone, needed, unneeded, push, pull, something, nothing, until my eyes no longer want any of it. As I start to fall asleep, I tell myself that I should let go of the idea that I'm supposed to be a mother already because I really don't have the energy to shake anyone off of me. And then Jena is saying that the best way to choose a nanny is to thump them like melons.

* * *

I'm outside in the hammock vowing to reconnect with my true self. Yesterday was a bust in terms of uncoiling the stress in my body. I woke up from my couch nap with a stiff neck and the realization that sleeping with headphones on was a safety hazard—there could have been a fire or a swarm of red ants. I spent the rest of the day repeatedly asking my brother if he was sure everything was okay, looking through all the cabinets for evidence of who-knows, convincing myself not to put my ear to the wall in search of insider celebrity gossip, being wide awake in the sleeping nook, eating individually wrapped foods, and, after dark, watching my other neighbor's comedy special—*Mick Brody: Here for It!*

Mick's jokes were sharp and meticulously rehearsed compared to Jena's half-awake conversational tone. His set was clever, sure, but also much less personal. All the jokes were told through the buffer of hypotheticals. *"What if our sex organs only functioned when our minds achieved a certain state? What if our crotch friends wouldn't work at all until we let the boundaries of the physical world fall away and truly understood that we're one with everything around us? Like, what if you had to deflate your ego to engage your libido? You'd have to meditate to masturbate. Zen it to win it. Turn off to get off. Imagine the effort! I think we could really get somewhere in terms of human harmony if this were the case . . . at least until some basement dude came up with a cheat code."*

I came away from Mick's special confused about whether I found him attractive and also about why my sex organs require so little of me, spiritually.

But today there will be no comedy specials. No, today I'm a hammock maiden with an ironclad mind-body connection.

I haven't heard a thing from Jena, Mick, or their child today. Success must lead to hard, deep sleep—no waking in the night to whisper *why not me?* And the child, who knows, maybe they give her cough syrup.

I call Neil and tell him I'm suspended in air near a power couple. He asks if the power couple is Janet Leigh and Tony Curtis, and I tell him that he turned grandpa really quickly, I am impressed. When I give him Jena and Mick's names, he's familiar and says their wedding ceremony famously doubled as a roast. The mic was passed around, and every guest had the opportunity to insult the bride and groom. Their flower girl called them talentless shitstains. Mick's mother stood up in the front row and said they were a perfect couple because Jena looked like a chainsaw and Mick looked like a tree stump. It's on YouTube, he says.

My brother and I agree that nothing is sacred anymore, but we disagree about whether this is for the better or the worse. I ask to talk to Grandpa, and Neil says he's sleeping. But it's 10:30 and he's never asleep at 10:30 and what the hell is going on over there? Neil is not worried. Grandpa said his head felt heavy, that's all.

That tracks. Grandpa and I often commiserate about our heavy heads while leaning against chairs. Puny necks and basic inability run in our family.

I ask if Grandpa slept last night, and Neil says sure.

I ask if he took all his pills, and Neil says every one.

I ask if, when taking the pills, Grandpa made the joke about this one makes me bigger and this one makes me smaller and this one takes me right down the rabbit hole, and Neil says yes, verbatim.

I'm considering asking Neil to wake Grandpa up so he can confirm that these were in fact his exact words when the child of the comedy couple appears at the side of my hammock and says she wants up.

I tell Neil I have to go, and I tell the child to scoot back because we aren't wearing masks. I read somewhere that young kids don't spread the virus as much, but that seems untrue—simply another way people discount the potency of children, like assuming they don't have sexualities or harbor ill will.

The child takes several steps back and tells me her name is Jilly, and I say thanks for letting me know, even though I'd already read her name, birth weight, and astrological sign on the internet. She's holding her long nightgown up above her belly and swishing it from side to side across her rib cage in a way that redefines the phrase "belly dancing." I swing my legs down and sit up, hoping to give myself more authority, and ask Jilly where her parents are.

The child tells me her parents are taking a shower and then puts her gown down, like she's given enough away. This feels neglectful on her parents' part. I know people with kids need to have sex (*especially* famous people since they must look freshly fucked at all times), but this child (age three?) seems too young to be left alone. I ask if she knows how to play Simon Says.

She says no but that she does know how to play quacker crackers, a game where you eat saltines while pretending to be a duck. I have no crackers so I go ahead and explain the rules of Simon Says, but I can tell I'm losing her interest and who can blame her because what authoritarian child-hater invented this game, anyway? I pivot, ask her if she wants to show me how long she can hop on one leg. She declines. Turns out it's hard to engage with a nonchalant child who must stay six feet away.

Then her mother is running toward us with wet hair. Jena seems genuinely worried and horrified, says Jilly was sleeping only a moment ago, that she left cartoons on in case she woke up, that she's never escaped before, that she's so thankful I was with her. Jena tries to hold Jilly against her body, reclaiming her as safe, but Jilly pushes her away, deciding that now is the time to hop on one foot.

Mick runs out from their side of the duplex and exhales when he sees his daughter, not only fine but hopping on her own terms. Jilly's parents both kneel down to her level and take turns trying to convince her that something serious has just happened. They are loving and patient and attractive, and I feel bad about judging them as bad parents while wondering, too, what sort of sex they just had, like who was where and which legs were bent.

When Mick and Jena stand up, I can tell they've gone from alarmed to relieved too quickly. They have that realigned priorities look, and I'm pretty sure they're about to start gushing thank yous and what-would-have-happeneds, which would make me uncomfortable because, really, I didn't do anything. So I quickly say hey, Jilly told me about quacker crackers, so cute.

Jena explains that Mick invented the game for Jilly when she was sad and snotty from a head cold and then leans over on him, like what a guy.

Mick puts his arm around Jena and says that really he's pretty crumby at that game, and I let out a big, squawky, genuine laugh. We all know this sound came out of me because Mick is slightly famous and medium-handsome, and I'm embarrassed by this transparency. I should have let them gush apologies and gratitude—uncomfortable beats embarrassed every time. I stand up to get myself away from what I might do next and say glad everything worked out, the hammock's all yours, have a good day. Jilly climbs into the hammock as soon as I'm out and Jena says thanks again and Mick says thank you so much Morgan, which is a name very very close to the one I told them yesterday.

* * *

Inside, I sit at the kitchen table and write the word "idiot" in bubble letters on an envelope I found stuffed between books on the shelf. Idiots should stay inside because idiots can't help but over-laugh when professional comics make minor-league puns. Idiots should only fraternize with grandpas who tend to shrug and grin at whatever they say, probably because those grandpas didn't even hear what was said.

When I was a child, my mother would pull me out of my shame spirals by setting the oven timer and letting me wallow in how unredeemable I felt for ten minutes and ten minutes *only*. I liked to spend those minutes bent in half, groaning and letting my hair touch the ground. When the timer went off, Mom would say enough and I'd stand back up and feel . . . not exactly redeemed but neutral and spent. If Mom were here, she'd remind me that being too hard on myself has cost me a lot already (by which she'd mean: a completed degree, a job with benefits, a signature style, a circle of friends, true love, a reliable sense of self, etc. and so on) so I shouldn't let it ruin my prepaid (by her) weekend as well.

But she's not here, so I fill in the letters I-D-I-O-T with dark ink and replay the cringey exchange over and over while sitting under a wooden moose plaque carved with the words "wild life."

* * *

By night, I'm over it. I'm so over it that I'm wearing a sheet mask and humming along to Doris Day. I have her music on my phone for Grandpa's benefit, but the songs turn out to be a wonderful soundtrack for self-forgiveness.

Someone is knocking at the door. I peel off my mask and set it on the coffee table, even though it's been seven minutes shy of the recommended rejuvenation time. Eye to peephole, there's Jena. I open the door and she's fully made up—eyes, lips, jewelry, outfit, go-time smile—standing back but saying a lot at once. She's sorry, this is tacky, this is so weird, but also kind of an emergency and they usually have a nanny and Jilly is honestly *always* asleep at this hour but today was a late nap day and she and Mick are actually headlining, I mean if you can call it that, but still, a pretty big opportunity for them, plus a legit good cause, and I seem *so* nice and normal and Jilly already likes me.

She's asking me to babysit. There's a virtual comedy show to benefit laid-off restaurant employees in the LA area, and she and Mick are both doing sets live from the duplex. The show starts in twenty minutes, and her child is still very much awake, so she's offering to Venmo me $500 if I can watch Jilly for two hours.

First I think, *No way, I'm finally luxuriating.* Then I think, *I can't say no, she's right here with her stage makeup on and no other options,* and then, as I slip back to the familiar feeling of discounting my own preferences, I think, *All I'm qualified to do is keep other people alive for short periods of time,* so I say, sure, bring her over.

Jena starts to hug me, remembers that we can't hug anymore, then puts her hands back down and tells me that I'm saving her life.

Ten minutes later, Jilly is in my side of the duplex. She's wearing the same nightgown as this morning but in a pale yellow, and she is carrying a paper napkin that she and her father have doodled all over with pen. She shows me the napkin while she's still inside the doorway, like she needs to prove to me, right away and with written evidence, that she belongs to the people on the *other* side of this building.

Her contributions to the napkin are crude x's and incomplete circles, and she identifies each one for me. That's a polar bear, that's my nanny's purse, that's a pond, that one I didn't mean to do so I marked it out, that's a balloon, that's a person who is falling, that's . . . that's just a line. Mick's pictures are charming, clearly drawn to make his daughter smile and to keep her occupied by something other than screens for ten or fifteen minutes. He drew funny cowboys, fuzzy kittens, a snake wearing a backpack. He's also written the words "Jilly," "Mama," and "Daddy." Jilly asks me if I want to write my name. I better not, I say, your parents think my name is Morgan.

We hear them laugh through the wall. The laughs sound real, maybe only slightly exaggerated for the fry cooks and waitstaff and franchise owner-operators. Jilly doesn't react to the sound of her parents. She takes off her jellies, sets them beside the door, places her napkin on top of them, and asks me what I like to play.

I ask her if she's ever flown on a plane, but of course she has, given her parentage and the fact that she owns one nightgown in several colors. Even so, she's thrilled when I lie down on the moose-colored carpet, hold her hands, put my feet to her belly, and let her fly up to the height of my outstretched legs. From my view, the ceiling is her backdrop, and she looks happy, like she's being taken care of, which makes me happy, which makes me a level of happy so much higher than I would have reached on my own here tonight.

* * *

Jilly fell asleep on my couch after I told her a story about two rocks who were thrown into a creek and became friends underwater on the creek bed, so maybe being thrown wasn't the worst thing that ever happened to them after all—which I worried had a moral dangerously close to *things happen for a reason*, but I was in too deep to change course.

Now I'm sitting in the dark near her bare feet wondering what I'll do with this $500 windfall. All my ideas involve spending it on Grandpa: reupholstering his orange chair, retuning his piano, remodeling his bathtub into a walk-in deal. I could buy him a lobster feast, like the one he had on his honeymoon. He loves to talk about those happy years with Grandma, when their contented love—and not his drinking—was the headline.

I get a text from Neil that says, *Thanks for doing this every day. Also how do you do this every day?* And all I can think to write back is, *I don't know how I do it but please take good care of him so I can keep doing it. I don't want to go back to pretending to work toward what I'm supposed to want,* so I don't respond at all.

Now Jena and Mick are at the window, peeking at us through cupped hands. I gesture for them to come in, the door's unlocked. I click on a lamp as they come in with their comedown energy. They've just gotten off stage, more or less, so they are buzzy and stumbly. I ask how it went, and she says he did great and he says she stole the show.

I tell them Jilly and I had a good time, that it was no problem at all, she's a great kid. I don't say she's such a sweet sleeper even though she is, I mean look at her.

Mick agrees about Jilly's greatness. He says that she is turning out to be so funny, but I promise that we didn't force her to be, that we'd have found it in our hearts to love a humorless child.

I'll miss spending all this extra time with her, Jena says, and Mick says yes, me too.

You mean when your trip is over? I ask.

Yeah, we can go home now, finally. I got a message during the show that our nanny Crista doesn't have Covid after all, Jena says. So we can go back to our house and Crista can take care of Jilly. Back to normal.

Jena explains that Crista had been exposed through her hairdresser, and since they had recently let Crista move in, which just made sense because she was at their house fifty hours a week anyway, they couldn't exactly kick her out to quarantine elsewhere. So they left instead.

This was the only rental we could find last-minute, Mick says. He looks around and adds: Though I'm kinda bummed that we didn't get the moose side. It's bear country over there.

But . . . wait . . . why didn't you mention this to me? I ask. What if Crista *had* been positive?

Jena says she had a gut feeling that the nanny didn't have it. Crista tends to exaggerate, I mean she says she's cried in *every* grocery store she's ever been in which . . . seems like a lot of crying and why wouldn't you stay in the car if you were that upset? Who's that hungry? She always plays things up. So when she said she saw this hairdresser the day before she tested positive, I figured it had been at least five days, so we were fine.

But you didn't know for sure, I say. You couldn't. And if she'd had the virus, you all could have been positive too. Jilly was in my living space, exhaling all over me! I can't get sick, I *live* with my *grandpa*! Who is old! You could have . . .

Instead of finishing my sentence about how they could have killed my best friend, I imagine grabbing their sleeping child's toe and twisting it hard in retribution for their carelessness.

Jena realizes that I'm truly upset, that I'm not letting this slide because they are so attractive and charming. She stands up a little straighter. We weren't thinking, we should have thought, I'm so sorry, this whole week has been . . . I'll pay you more than the $500, okay? she says.

I don't answer about the money. I'm thinking instead about the stories of people with the virus dying alone, with no one, and about how Grandpa has spent the last twenty-five years staying sober, making amends, asking my mom and her brothers for forgiveness, finally listening, admitting wrong, and how if he got sick, he'd have to die completely on his own, like he hadn't been forgiven at all.

Mick scoops up Jilly's limp body and tells me that he is sorry about this and I can recklessly endanger *his* grandpa if that would make me feel better, maybe take his gramps out on a motorcycle ride, plop him into my sidecar without a helmet, and then accelerate as I merge onto the freeway and then whatever happens, happens . . .

I bite my cheeks to keep from smiling, because sidecar grandpa bits are right up my alley, and tell Mick that not everything is some joke, that something awful and irreversible could have happened, that my name is MEGAN, that I am going to tell them the right thing to do in this situation since they clearly don't know how to do the right thing. What they are going to do, I say, is give me enough money to have my grandpa's porch screened in so he can sit out in the sunshine without getting eaten up by mosquitos, because he shouldn't have to worry about welts and discomfort when all he wants is to feel some warmth on his skin and to be reminded of easier times, of better times. I tell them that would be the right thing to do here, the unselfish thing.

All I Need Are These Four Walls and Some Positive Feedback

Treatie is a second-generation Delightico confectioner. Actually, she's probably the thousandth-something generation, if you go back to the rainforest where her mother was captured and dig into the time and bones you might find there. But she is the second generation to make confections for a company, for placement in plastic wrappers, for global distribution.

Treatie looks like a furry Cabbage Patch baby in a Miss Piggy wig and lives alone in a small room with a hammock and a deep sink. She doesn't brush her fur at all because she is a wild animal, even if she was born in a room with artificial lighting and minor conveniences. Sometimes she likes to sleep in the sink and lick her paws clean in the hammock to prove to herself that she's not fully domesticated. *See*, she thinks, *I have options and preferences and some of them are wet and wild.*

Today, like all her days, will mostly be spent on the floor. To make the round two-inch patties the world requires of her, Treatie has to lie on her side, put her wrists together above her head, and concentrate on the idea that something can come from nothing. She pictures, of course, the stock image of creation—new plants poking through the soil—but she also thinks of concrete pouring from the drum of a massive mixer, heads escaping fully dilated cervixes, cells dividing evenly, Polaroid cameras ejecting square photos, the first squeal of a baby piglet, mold forming inside jars of pesto, time-lapsed worms regrowing the section of body they lost, steam rising from dryer vents on the exterior of a brick house, a hair popping up at the exact midpoint between two eyebrows.

She does what she's told during the daylight—always meeting or exceeding her output quotas—but at night she can use her claws to scratch up the Formica if she wants to. In the morning, she thinks these claw marks look like they came from a creature who wants to escape, which troubles her because she loves her one good home.

(Further evidence of her animal heart: she occasionally makes the sound she knew how to make without ever being taught. The sound is nearly a shriek but more rumbly and guttural. And it loops and repeats, like the sound is chasing its own tail. Once a brown bug got into Treatie's room, and when she saw the bug's many legs moving across her floor, this ancient pre-installed sound came out of her, and the bug fell on its back and died of horror.)

Midmorning, as instructed, she gets off the floor to check her tablet for comments and messages from her chocolate fans. The tablet was made especially for her, meaning it's claw-operated and bigger than her sink. (She classifies all objects as either "smaller than the sink" or "bigger than the sink" because her sink is one of the only objects she's experienced firsthand.) Even without the right kind of voice box for speaking, Treatie has the written vocabulary of a twelve-year-old, thanks to the daily lessons she received during her youth involving flash cards and motivational papaya chunks.

The replies *"So glad you enjoyed it"* and *"Of course I'm real!"* work for nearly all of her photo comments, which are overwhelmingly positive. She once saw a comment that said *"This shit tastes like melted pantyhose,"* but it disappeared right away, so Treatie convinced herself that what it actually said was *"Shit, this tastes like melted paradise."* This morning she posts a picture of her hair flipped in front of her face and captions it: *"Treatie is here, or is she?* KIDDING. *Peekaboo and keep yourselves way too sweet today, babyfriends."*

Then back to the floor, to production. She tries to mix up the creation montage, shuffle shuffle, to keep her awe fresh and her flavors potent. The shuffling comes naturally because she was given a tablet that played a video compilation of these images as soon as she was old enough to hold an object up to her face. They (the handlers, the execs, the humans who kept her room clean and stocked) called this tablet her treat. When she wanted to nurse and nuzzle her mother, to fall asleep near that familiar warm belly, they told her no, get up, get back, Mother needs to work, to produce, but here, she could have her treat instead. She once threw the tablet against the wall and cracked the screen, and that's when they settled on calling her Treatie, rudely naming her after her own refusal.

(Treatie learned about regurgitating tree frogs and the way the darkness of nighttime swallows the forest from her mother, who could make Delighticos without video inspiration. Treatie has tried to incorporate these secondhand memories into her candy-making, but since she has no visual reference—and since her mother is no longer there to further describe them—they make her Delighticos come out flat, like graham crackers, and sharp, like vinegar.)

Slowly, if she focuses on what she can actually picture, and if the wrist rubbing and the mental conjuring are quick enough, the Delightico begins to form between Treatie's wrists. The center appears first: a tiny ball of almond paste and coconut nougat, then a layer of caramel, then the crunchy cookie shell, and last the chocolate, which comes out of her accompanied by euphoria and the thought *this is for me*. Then she immediately gives it away, placing the confection on a wire rack with the others—ready to be packaged, boxed, and driven toward the people who don't really believe she exists outside of some marketer's imagination. But all Treatie knows is that her comments are truly *overwhelmingly* positive.

She makes seven more Delighticos, then checks for new comments. The first one reads: *"R you sloth?"* Right then one of her handlers comes in with two spiky pineapple crowns for her to gnaw on. He asks her if she needs her litter box changed (yes, please) and reminds her, once again, not to post any more pictures of her sink. Enough is enough, he says.

When he leaves, Treatie goes back to find the comment. She's never been compared to a sloth before. A spider? Often. But never a sloth. (One of Treatie's first video montages contained a spider spinning a web, and yes, she sees the resemblance in terms of process but not, thankfully, in terms of physicality.) But since she's never seen a sloth, she can't know for sure if she, in fact, R *sloth*.

She reads the question again, and it makes her feel overheated, like the thickness of her fur has doubled. All her other comments express sentiments more like yum, yummy, or yummers. She notices that the sink photo she posted yesterday has been taken down. Treatie is hurt by this because she was only trying to give the drain its due. She wishes her account wasn't so curiously slippery, that words and pictures would stay where she put them.

In order to answer the question in an informed way, she types the word "sloth" in the search bar of her photo-sharing app, knowing this will put her behind in her production schedule. And just like that, she's looking at squares and squares of creatures who look like they could be her mother's baldheaded cousins. Six, twelve, twenty-four, thirty thousand, endless cousins. Not exact matches—their heads are more squashed, less round, and their limbs are longer and meatier, and of course the lack of long, flowing hair—but she can tell these are relatives, the most family she's had in some time. She uses her claws to stroke the pictures, especially the wet snouts, where the resemblance to her mother is strongest.

There's a sloth hanging upside down with what appears to be a dopey smile and the caption: "A sloth's main goal is to conserve energy. They move at a leisurely pace and hold off on their poops until the very last minute." *Oh, maybe we aren't alike after all*, Treatie thinks as she moves back to the floor to make more Delighticos. *I'm a mover and a shaker. I keep a tight schedule and have never even considered delaying my poops.*

But that night, quota met, she finds that someone has answered the sloth question. For her. As her. *"Sloth? Not even close! But keep your eyes peeled for the reveal of my new Happy Easter packaging. Hope you like pastels!"* For the first time, she makes the connection between her sink pics being deleted and her handlers' hatred of her sink pics.

But that night, she tries chewing her dinner extra slowly, breathing through the rushed pace that normally propels her, and swallowing only when the food is fully mushed. For the first time in years, there's a pause to her constant stomach ache.

But that night, she hangs upside down from the underside of her hammock instead of sleeping in its dip, and for the first time her dreams are right-side up.

* * *

The next morning she makes zero Delighticos. She counts her breaths and watches the lines in the tiled floor. She pictures her identical counterparts out there in the untiled wild, out there being still in the trees, and tries to sync herself up with a pace that doesn't recognize the word "output."

After doing the most nothing she's ever done, after forcing her mind to slow down enough to mull things over, she decides to post the photo with the hair over her face again but with these new words: *"I would never say that I am not even close to a sloth because I am really plenty close. Check the snouts. My mother, she remembered swinging from trees and a certain orange berry that was worth the climb. The point is, they are writing to you pretending to be me. They are deleting my posts, and they will probably delete this one too. So listen, I slept upside down last night, and my limbs loved it. Listen, they told me my mother would be right back. Listen, I can no longer stand to picture all that something coming from all that nothing. Listen, I can make this wild sound, for real. You won't believe it. See my stories for video proof, sound UP."*

As soon as she posts, someone tries to open her door. But they don't know that she's taken her hammock down and is ready to use it as a capture net, they don't know how much the Formica has sharpened and strengthened her claws, they don't know that last night she opened wide and took a picture of her canines to confirm their shape and capabilities, they don't know what her fans will do on her behalf, or about the real power of "brand loyalty."

No Space Is Too Small When
Your Head Is Detachable

I look out my window more than I should, but that's only because I believe that most people are up to something. I think *aha* even before I part the blinds. *Aha, I caught you picking your wedgie or your nose while failing to pick up after your dog.* Or, *Aha, you're busted. I see the way you're leering at those porch packages. You want to nab them; your stupid heart hopes they contain small electronics even though we both know you're going to end up with a month's supply of pet kibble.*

I work from home. I live alone.

It's possible that I'm lonely but not for anyone I've met so far.

I really shouldn't have my desk right by the window, but I moved it to the far wall once before and wore myself out walking back and forth every time I heard a horn or a footstep or a prolonged silence.

I'm actually a wonderful neighbor. Thoughtful. Attentive. When the guy across the street had his third wife leave him and his second heart attack in the same week, I set a bag of sweet potatoes at his door with a note that said, "If you want me to mow your lawn, let me know by Thursday afternoon because I'll have to rearrange my weekend plans." And on Halloween I give out those Tootsie Roll tubes that can be used as piggy banks once they're empty. So I'm giving the kids immediate happiness with the twisted-up sugar but also future happiness when their nickels clink up up up.

This morning I can't get the daily cash flow spreadsheet to come out right. I'm off by a factor of nine—so I know I've transposed two numbers—but spending forty minutes looking for a split-second slip-up of my index finger makes me wonder if the life I'm living is worth all that diaper-changing my parents put in.

I eventually find the mixed-up digits. Seven and nine, odd fucks. And then I hear the bike crew. Always so shouty, the bike crew—something about pedaling their legs makes these neighborhood kids feel the need to go full volume. There are typically only five or six of them, but at any given moment two of them are yelling, "Wait for me!" The group tends to roam unsupervised, but when there's a wreck or a shoving match, parents materialize with antibiotic ointments and long, straight arms to break up tussles. I'm happy to see *any* sort of parental responsibility in this neighborhood, even if it comes post-blood, too late.

I look down at the sidewalk, but no, the children still aren't cute. Too old, too determined to be active. But they all wear cartoon animal T-shirts, so maybe they know they need the boost in cuteness.

They ride past twelve times (according to the tally on this Post-it), and right when I've learned to incorporate their twice-a-minute noise parade into my work mindset, they stop. I peek out right away but not—I can assure you—out of concern. *Anyone* who's made double-digit tally marks about something can't help becoming invested in an outcome.

They've stopped next door at Laurabeth's house. Looks like today is shaping up to be her yard junk day, based on the motorcycle helmet (and what is that, a meat grinder?) on her lawn. I don't know if Laurabeth is a hoarder, but she clearly likes to hold onto things. Her house is packed wall-to-wall with stuff she can't even sit on or screw light bulbs into. Her adult children made her promise she'd get rid of eight items a month, so they'll be left with that much less mess when she's gone. And once she hits age seventy-five she has to up it to twelve items a week. Speed round. So every so often she has a casual yard sale—one without a sign or price stickers, one where she has to grasp her porch railing with both hands to keep from grabbing her belongings back from the looky-loos.

The bike crew love Laurabeth's giveaways, though I'm certain they don't know what most of the items are. Last month I watched a six-year-old in a tankini drag a leaf blower home.

One of the kids is cranking the meat grinder while the others cheer. How obscene. Laurabeth comes back out with a fireplace poker, a throw pillow, three rulers, and a box of tampons. I wonder what her offspring would say about her counting the rulers as three separate items instead of bundling them into one. Smells like a workaround to me, Laurabeth.

Right away the blond twins go for the tampons. I am sure they'll scratch each other's eyes out, but instead they work together to open the box and pass tampons out to the crowd, like celebratory cigars. A ruler sword fight breaks out, but the kid with the fireplace poker ends it. Laurabeth goes inside, maybe because she doesn't want to be responsible for any of the eyeball damage that feels increasingly likely.

The children's pockets are full of tampons, so they look pretty stupid—but also pretty rich. Someone grinds a tampon through the meat grinder. Someone is comically pregnant with a throw pillow. The littlest one (in skinny jeans despite still being baby-shaped) sits down in the motorcycle helmet and turns it into a fun seat by spinning it around.

Too many free thrills going on down there. Too much mess. And now they, as a group, are knocking on Laurabeth's door. When she opens up, one asks, "Can we have more?" and I don't hear her answer because I am already heading downstairs to talk to them about propriety. By the time I get there, Laurabeth is hauling out a tall metal cabinet with some difficulty. I yell at the two biggest children to stop standing there, to grab the bottom of the cabinet. As the three of them maneuver down the porch steps, I pick decimated tampon out of the grass and tell the kid in skinny jeans that they better not potty in that helmet.

There's an argument about who will take the cabinet home. Someone wants to store their Lego collection in it. Someone wants to fill it with potatoes and water them until they sprout long eyes. Someone's thinking of Mother's Day, of painting it yellow for her. I tell Laurabeth to go rest, that I'll clean up the mess. I tell the children that whoever takes the cabinet will need an adult and maybe a truck, and they scatter to find the closest adult and the quickest truck.

The rulers are gone, but I lay the fire poker on the pillow and turn the helmet over, respectfully. A real person could use these, the kind of person who's done growing. I start to go back home, but then I get curious about whether I'd fit into the metal cabinet. I have a small frame, my hips are bendy, my head is practically detachable. I try it, and I do fit. It's tight, but I can close the door. I wonder how long until a kid comes to claim this thing. I wonder why I'm in here. I wonder if I want to scare someone—say boo, say stop, say this isn't yours, not everything is for you—or if what I really want is to join the crew who move their legs fast and take what they want and aren't very cute at all.

Babies Don't Keep

I packed my blue kiddie-sized suitcase that said "Off to Grandma's House." In went the socks that I liked to roll down into ankle worms. In went the hairbrush with my spelling bee name tag stuck on the handle to claim it as mine—just like the dark greasy hair wound through it.

Usually the suitcase referred to my dark-haired grandma's because that's where I took it. This time I was packing for a trip to my red-haired grandma's, but the suitcase was still right about where I was headed.

I put in a wax air freshener shaped like a teddy bear. The bear wore blue jeans, and I'd melted his head into his shoulders with a lamp light. I meant to—had wished for a real flame and quicker dripping. The bear was a victim but still smelled like sea breeze. I always sniffed my victim before going to sleep. Routines were secretly holding me together.

I hoped my mom would pack a bag for my sister. Without help, her bag would be only Tootsie Rolls, trolls, and hard objects for pelting me when I most deserved it. No underwear, just projectiles.

I finished packing my suitcase hours before I was to be taken anywhere. I sat on my bed with my shoes buckled and looked in the mirror and saw the kind of girl who packed her bag hours early and then put on her shoes and looked in the mirror and watched herself pat-pat her bag to make sure it was staying ready.

I watched Grandma pull up through my sheer curtains. She parked her tan Buick, put her purse on her shoulder, then, remembering she was in a small town where purse snatchings were rare and she could acquire her granddaughters for free, set her purse back down.

My mom let me open the door. Grandma was no longer her mother-in-law, so Mom was under no obligation to smile, coo, or offer pigs-in-a-blanket when she came around. Mom put out her cigarette and placed both feet on the floor—she no longer needed to impress, but that didn't mean she wanted to be caught all bunched up and puffing away.

"Look at you, all ready to go! I guess you didn't have time to brush your hair. Where's your sister?" Grandma stood there fragrant and put together, masterfully middle-aged. She was the only person in my life who wore outfits and not just clothes. This gave her a certain authority over my hair. Her go-to look was bright, multi-colored tops tucked into solid slacks, plus jazzy belts, beaucoup jewelry, a crisp hairdo, shoulder purse, and foo-foo perfume. She had a high, slim waist, and it seemed like her whole past and future revolved around that fact— her middle being so easy to locate.

Grandma looked past me and saw my mom sitting up straight and not on fire. "How are you doing, Mandy?"

Mom said she was "getting along fine," but did not offer examples of her fineness or ask any questions in return. Instead she got up to see what was keeping my sister from getting this woman off her porch.

I was telling Grandma that I'd packed a swimsuit just-in-case when we heard yelling.

"It's time to go. Right now!"

"I want to bring the whole thing!"

"You can't! It doesn't fit in your bag! Just take everything from inside and pack it. Same thing."

Grandma and I heard a scream that started upright then dropped to the floor. Then we heard the brown carpet take some abuse from Tara's fists and heels. I was glad, really, because that carpet deserved it. I bet Grandma wished she had her purse to look through while she stood through this tantrum—she could have feigned gum-rifling to break the tension.

I told her, "I better go see what's going on."

She looked in at our couch and said, "I guess I'll wait in the car."

When I walked in, Tara was still pounding, and my mom had her face in her hands. Mom saw me and offered, "She wants to bring her entire drawer."

Tara stopped moving and crying so that her justification wasn't coming from an out-of-control animal. "I need to bring it because Chomp-Chomp sleeps in there. It's her bed!"

Chomp-Chomp was my sister's stuffed rabbit, whom I'd never ever seen sleep anywhere other than in Tara's twin bed, in the crook of her arm. I said, "Why can't she bring the drawer?"

"Because . . . it's part of the dresser."

"We will bring it back." I made it into a "we" situation, like the idea was gathering momentum. *Practically everyone thinks bringing the whole drawer is a reasonable idea.*

Tara looked at me to forgive me for about 20 percent of how I'd treated her up until that moment. I had to keep her tipped slightly toward me with these moments of understanding so she didn't hit me *too* hard when she hit me too hard.

Mom said, "It's heavy. And what would your grandma think?"

From the floor Tara watched to see if I was pulling for her strong enough to get past the next, logistical hurdle.

"We'll tell her it's a Reed family tradition—that your family has traveled with their dresser drawers for centuries. One guy started it, and then that became the way it was done. Like how Johnny Appleseed's descendants probably still wear pots on their heads."

Tara put her ankle on her opposite knee and said "yeah" like she'd just been taking a casual floor rest or doing a yoga pose and not wigging out about a detachable piece of furniture.

Mom must have realized how close she was to being free from us for two days. "Fine. But I'm not carrying it out to her car. You two will have to manage." She gave us each a kiss on the cheek, went into her room, and shut the door.

As Tara and I lugged the drawer across the lawn, we remarked conspiratorially on how light it was, really, and how well Chomp-Chomp would sleep in the city. Grandma popped the trunk without comment. We didn't even have to tell her about the Reed tradition; she could tell by our unkempt hair that we came with a fair amount of straggly reasoning.

* * *

Tara and I rode in the backseat because Grandma had plastic shopping bags in the front and didn't offer to move them. Also, we needed to be close enough to fight and huff at each other without getting cricks in our necks.

Grandma never asked about school or friends or if we'd been nice to Mommy. She wanted to spend time with *us*, not with a five- and a seven-year-old. She knew our day-to-day lives were boring struggles and that nothing that happened at school was worth sharing, so instead she told us about her life.

I was glad I didn't have to produce answers like, "Yes, my teacher is very nice, she grades our papers in green instead of red," but I *did* want to tell someone about getting under my desk for earthquake drills in my dress, how cold the concrete floor felt on my underwear when I leaned back into a crouch. And about my daily work digging out tree roots at recess. Every day I exposed more tendrils, and every day I became less articulate.

Grandma told us about selling high-end stuffed animals to rich children and the parents who wanted to shut them up, and about her new dummy cat who tried to sleep on the wrought iron headboard, repeatedly falling into the crack between the bed and the wall with a squawk like, *I thought this time would be different!*

I filed away all this incoming information. I looked like a blank, incapable child who might sit watching the house flies fly, but I was a Rolodex in cotton tights. All the info I took in, including these new stories, might contain clues I'd need someday when I learned how to be a person.

Tara looked out the window. This made me furious. I wanted to hurt her so that I didn't have to think about how *she* saw the world when I was busy with my own investigation.

I whispered to her, "You smell like Mom when she first wakes up."
She frowned, hurt and small, and tried to kick me.

Grandma said, "Stop that fighting or you won't get to see what's in
these bags."

Tara stopped so I gave her a victorious look, because even though
we both stood to gain from the bags, she had already sustained my
critical comment while I remained unkicked.

Tara told Grandma that we'd each gotten a puppy from a neighborhood litter. Spunk, the puppy she'd chosen, was still alive and chasing
cars while the dog I'd chosen, Lucky, was killed by a car just as soon as
I'd named him. Tara said, "Isn't that kind of funny? Lucky?"

And Grandma laughed because it was kind of funny when you
weren't the owner and the namer of the unlucky pup. So Tara kicked
me back without compromising the bag of goodies, and while I stewed
about the comedic, deflating death of my pet I was also relieved that my
sister had tipped us back to even. I did my best damage in retribution.

* * *

We'd been driving for two hours when we stopped at a gas station.
Grandma needed to fill up and said we could get a snack, which meant
candy because we weren't the kind of girls to walk out with a bag of
pretzels.

Tara and I stayed in the car while Grandma pumped. We wordlessly
watched Grandma push buttons while the back of her belt sparkled
for us. When she turned around with the nozzle she tapped it on the
window, like a fun-loving warning. *Give me a smile with your hands
up where I can see 'em.*

Inside the gas station, I found the candy aisle and decided to get
Sixlets, which are like rounder M&M's, with even more of that factory-
made taste (bouquet of dye, notes of clanking).

Before I could finalize my choice by swiping it off the rack, I saw a
man in the next aisle. He was in the salt aisle: chips, peanut butter crackers, jerky sticks, mixed nuts. He held a bag of Funyuns, and I recognized
him immediately. If I hadn't been with Grandma I might not have

made such swift connections. I might have thought, *Bus driver? Farm hand? Yoyo's Pop-Pop?* But in that context I easily remembered that he had once been my low-level, temporary, menacing grandpa. An image of him reclining on the couch leering and sneering in pajama pants made my stomach grasp at my inner-skin for balance and composure.

I froze and tried to understand the implications of this sighting and whether I wanted to be recognized by this man. I scanned for Tara. She was safe with Grandma and the cold drinks. I considered army-crawling to them, but I knew the Sixlets would make me a conspicuous rattlesnake.

He hadn't noticed me yet. Then I recalled how unremarkable and forgettable a child I was. People *never* remembered me. I had to be formally introduced to my great-grandmother each holiday and every picnic. I could probably do a cha-cha dance with several packages of Sixlets and this past-grandpa wouldn't even look up.

This was a relief. This grandpa had, for a brief time, been the partner of my red-haired grandma, who was now only feet away with the cold drinks. I didn't know if they had been married or simply boyfriend and girlfriend, but I think they lived together. His razor and comb had been in her bathroom with her seashell art and her round cakes of pink soap.

I'd only picked up slivers about their relationship. From listening to adult conversations I'd learned that he'd been stealing from Grandma and had done the same with other women, that he'd pushed a girlfriend down concrete steps, that he'd gone by other names, that he was bad inside—wanting and taking. All while smelling too strongly of sharp pine. But the final point of all the slivers I'd gathered was this: she'd gotten away from him.

Until then. When he loomed one aisle over with his Funyuns. I wanted to sound an alarm and *be* an alarm. I didn't want to be unremarkable but ultra-remarkable, like a swirling flame that screams in beeps.

"Hey! Hey you! You're my grandbaby! Ain't you my little grandbaby?"

He was looking over and down at me, identifying me correctly. Except I was *never* his, and he knew me from ages five to six, when I could read and shower alone and wear bodysuits—so *not* a baby.

I decided not to speak but to cower. So much for being an alarm, for swirling in response to danger. In the heat of the moment I was all prey, all rabbit, begging for mercy only with my eyes.

"You are my grandbaby ain't ya? You've grown. You're gettin' lady legs!"

He was leaning on the rack between us and studying me like his eyes were the sun and I grew into a woman only under his edifying watch. I didn't know he was drunk, but I knew he was loose in a way that meant anything could happen. And that the "anything" felt tipped toward bad and toward irrevocable.

He knew I was scared, and this only brightened his beam. I heard my grandma's shoes tipping across the store. I saw her approach, looking only right at me because she'd had previous experience with his mean and binding focus.

She stopped at the entrance to my aisle. "Come on over here."

She was my well-dressed embassy. Tara was at her side, looking frightened and like she forgave me for another 20 percent of my awful behavior because she disliked seeing me in a vulnerable situation.

"Well, looky here. Pretty Miss Dreena. Here with our grandbabies. Looking so nice."

Grandma did not acknowledge him or meet his eye, and I understood, then, all the strength she had in her—her strength in that moment and in the moment she finally kicked him out of her house, in the moments I couldn't quite imagine yet, like what bad men did when they had the chance, and also in moments I was not privy to, moments from way before I was born, like when she was ten and an older neighbor boy pushed her down, lifted her skirt, and stood over her because he wanted her to know he could do more if he wanted, and in *that* moment her strength kept the truth of that powerlessness from penetrating her being.

I took my Sixlets and went to Grandma. She held my hand and led us to the checkout. She looked straight ahead, but Tara and I were weaker and watched him following us.

"Where are my three beautiful girls heading tonight?"

Two people were in front of us in line. Grandma gripped our skulls and turned our heads away from him.

"Where are you taking my grandbabies?" His voice was becoming more threatening and more cajoling.

I started to cry. It felt like he could do whatever he wanted since he'd claimed me as his grandbaby. Grandma pulled me into her hip. We were next in line.

Tara saw my tears and turned back to yell, "We are *not* your grandbabies! And you smell like your mom when she *first* wakes up!"

He laughed and he came closer, both actions that made my tears come harder. Grandma had to yank the Sixlets from my upset hand to pay for them. He was right beside us, nearest to me. He called Grandma's name. He called her "little wife." He asked where we were going over and over.

The woman behind the counter said, "Is there a problem here?" and I wanted to scream an affirmative and scramble behind the counter with her, back with the telephones and the guns and the propriety. But Grandma very coolly said we were fine, closed her purse, and handed us our candy.

She looked us in our eyes and said, "We are going to walk to the car and drive away."

I just knew he'd follow us and scratch at my window until he saw that none of my haughty confidence remained. I knew he wanted to put his yellow teeth in my face and feed off my disgust. But once we started toward the door, he stopped shouting and simply let us go. We got in and we drove away, just like Grandma said. I looked out the window at the gas station. He hadn't emerged. He wasn't chasing us.

We were not his grandbabies.

As she pulled back onto the road Grandma asked, "Are you girls okay?"

As Tara said, "No," I said, "He didn't even remember my name."

Internal
Riots

Secrets and Lies

Prove It

I got this job by pretending to be my long-dead, long-faced great-aunt. The credentials I listed are my own—I took the tests and got the degree. But my natural personality is more forlornly fault-finding than therapeutic, so during counseling job interviews I channel Aunt Renata, who called me "a beacon of God's love" even after I stole her Lincoln Town Car and got pregnant in it.

When I sat down with the director of Sun Porch Retirement Village I talked about goodness and redemption, and I never once mentioned worthiness or bad apples. I put my legit GPA in bold on my resume and then glanced down at it frequently during the interview to embolden myself and my ability to do an impression of a forgiving spirit who believes people are capable of change.

The facility director, Quinetta, asked me if I had experience working with the elderly.

"Oh, yes," I said. "In high school I worked at a truck stop, and there was a table of older men who never left. They sat in the corner near the bathroom, and I always gave them real decaf when they asked for it. Some of the other gals secretly served them regular because they didn't want to brew a whole new pot. But even then I knew that older people should be listened to and that their specific needs should not be ignored."

I didn't tell her that I was, in truth, one of the gals giving them caffeinated coffee because brown is brown or that I whole-heartedly despised that table of guys who called me "Come 'Ere" and who never left tips since they never left, period.

I also told Quinetta about one of my supervised practicum session clients—a twitchy, tender woman going through the change of life. When she couldn't sleep at night she went out into her van and pretended to honk the horn. She didn't want her car's midnight tooting to wake anyone, so she just brought her fist really close to the horn over and over until she felt two notches better. I told the client that was fine.

And now, thanks to this fine caliber of edited anecdotes, plus my good grades and my natural capabilities with demeanor-mimicry and tone-séance, I will start my job as Sun Porch's group counselor tomorrow morning. I aim to help people connect with their inner truths and with each other. I aim to nod more than I speak, to convey compassionate empathy with my eyeballs, and to always pull out of that parking lot by 4:45.

* * *

For my first day of work I wear a belted dress, white with a printed pattern of yellow flowers. The white is to symbolize surrendering to the process, the yellow is a nod to fear—whether the deep-seated or the yet-to-arise—and the belt is to draw eyes to my darling waist, which remains steadfastly defined even as the flesh above and below it expands and contracts like an inflatable kiddie pool in summer then winter then summer then winter.

Quinetta leads me into the dining hall and introduces me to the breakfast eaters. I see pink plastic plates in various states of undress and constellations of eyeglasses reflecting the overhead light. "Everyone, this is Candice Verlaine. As of today, she is our new counselor. She's extremely qualified and experienced, and I'd like you all to give her a warm welcome."

The residents hold their applause and greetings. They continue chewing and forking—most had stopped looking our direction even before Quinetta said the word "today." One man at a back table is holding up his cup of orange juice, but I don't know whether he is toasting my arrival or asking for a refill.

Quinetta clears her throat and says, "Candice deserves your respect and your genuine participation. We are giving this counseling program one last try, but if you . . . She's here to help . . . Let her help. Please."

She then grabs me by the elbow and pulls me down a hall and away from the dining area before I can make a determination about the intentions of OJ man, on which, I feel certain, my fate hinges.

Quinetta directs us into a room that has a preschool feel but with chairs made to accommodate bigger, higher butts. "This is the multipurpose room. Anything can happen in here! This is where you'll be spending a lot of your time."

I stare at a papier-mâché foot that hangs from the ceiling. It has been painted green, and the sole bears the words "walk on." I look at Quinetta's hair and ask, "What did you mean about this being the last chance for my program?" Her hair contains several bobby pins, and I feel entitled to one of them, maybe because of her information withholding, but I don't touch them.

She gestures to the chairs at the nearest table, where someone has carved the word "rules" into the tabletop. As we sit, Quinetta says, "We've tried to implement the group counseling program twice before. First we had a nice woman, right out of school, whom residents wouldn't speak to at all. She'd get the participants in a circle and ask them to bring their vulnerability to the circle with them, and there they'd sit—round and mum. Just a lot of shifty eye contact and lip licking. She quit the second day in tears, saying she felt like the star of a reality TV show about institutions that was also a horror movie about humanity's inability to connect.

"After she left, I took different residents aside and tried to understand why they refused to participate. They told me (each in their own way) that they didn't appreciate a woman their grandkids' age trying to tell them how to live, seeing as her experience with living was pretty paltry. I explained that she wasn't telling them *how* to live, she was only asking them to talk about the life they'd lived so far, to get to the deep truth of it all. And Candice, every time I said the word 'truth' there would be a physical reaction from the person I was talking to—they'd bug their eyes or snort or fiddle around with a shirt button. It's like the truth was on strike and the counselor was a scab, crossing the picket line.

"On the second go-around we went another direction. We hired an older man—closer to their age—who had more of an authoritarian vibe. We thought they'd consider him harder to defy, like maybe he'd remind them of their belt-wielding principal. And sure enough, they talked to him *plenty*. On his first day they went on and on about their father's long hours at the chicken plant or how their grandma slapped them for putting a fork with the spoons. They told these stories in great detail and talked all about how it made them feel. *When my daughter gave me a Dustbuster for my birthday twenty years ago, I felt like she was saying it was time for me to start cleaning up my own messes. That, and because she stopped bringing me bottles from the liquor store.* That kind of thing. Or, *When I caught my husband of forty years standing in a public fountain fondling a nude statue, I knew it was time for us to rekindle our physical relationship.*

"But by day two, the giggling started. The stories had gotten even more far-fetched. One of them said he'd always had a sexual fantasy about being boiled into a harder version of himself, like an egg. No one could keep a straight face. It became clear that it was all a performance, that they'd banded together to give us the only truth they could part with—blatant lies.

"Honestly, I think they did get *some* benefit from working together on their little show. I know better than to downplay the health effects of laughing in a group. I was willing to let it continue as a tall-tale contest since my ultimate goal was to boost morale, but the gentleman counselor thought it beneath him to nod along to manufactured emotions. What's funny is that I think the young woman, the first counselor, would have gone along with this pretend-therapy arrangement. It's hard to make situations align, isn't it? But that's my job. As director."

Quinetta has been talking for a long time, and I have fallen into a sinkhole of regret. I don't want this job. I'm used to being without health insurance. I'm *good* at being without health insurance, even—when I

sprained my wrist I fashioned a homemade cast out of packing tape
and two menstrual pads, which are offered free-of-charge in the public
restroom near the outdoor tennis courts. This job isn't worth the head-
ache. I look Quinetta in the eye and say, "I served them regular coffee.
The table of older guys, I dosed them with caffeine."

She smiles at me like I'm a child who made marker dots all over
her skin in a ploy to stay home from school. "Too late," Quinetta says.
"Your first group starts in half an hour."

***

I've been in the bathroom for twenty minutes. Stalling in the stalls.
The yellow flowers on my dress look more yellow than they did at
home—it's either the fluorescent lighting or the amplification of the
fear they represent.

I try again with my self-centering pep talk. *Okay so . . . I am about
to lead a counseling session for a group of people who denigrate the truth.
How fitting it is that I lied to get this job. How touching. How easy it is
for situations to align.*

I need to land on a tactic or a strategy before heading into the
multi-purpose room for the session. Should I acknowledge the past
antics right away? Should I give them a fresh start, a clean slate, a blank
stare? Perhaps I should walk in with threats and belittlement. Maybe
I should open with a song.

Someone outside the bathroom calls out, "Ma'am, are you still in
there?"

I do not answer. I am a liar, not a bathroom hollerer. I leave the stall,
wash my hands, and exit the bathroom to find a man and his cleaning cart. The cart holds a mop and full rolls of individually wrapped
TP. He eyes my waist and says, "Sorry, but . . . I saw you go in and I've
been waiting for you to come out for quite a long time."

His face tells me that this is more patience than he offers most and
that I ought to be both grateful and sorry. Meanwhile, the wet blue
loops of the mop come up to his shoulder, making him look like he
has a depressed Raggedy Andy for a conjoined twin. I say, "If you must

know, I have a *nasty* UTI. My doctor said she hasn't seen a case this bad since Elizabeth Taylor."

He laughs, and I wince at the friendliness of the sound. He was supposed to be stunned, not amused. "Wow," he says, "which stall were you in, lady? Maybe I should scrub it extra."

I've inadvertently opened myself up to banter. My UTI line was intended to be a conversation-ender, not an open invitation to a chat-and-cackle. It's my fault; I went too specifically absurd by referencing a dead celeb.

I point my thumb back at the door. "The one closest to the hand dryer. I hope you have bleach." I walk away quickly before he can volley back a response with the corresponding level of wit. I make sure my shoes clack the floor in self-assured tones, and I try not to wonder if, perhaps, something about this building enfeebles my ability to lie in a way that gets me what I want.

* * *

The participating residents are already in a circle when I enter the room. They've pushed the tables back and brought the chairs forth. I'm waylaid from the start, as the only line I'd rehearsed back in the stall was, "Let's form a circle."

They've not left me an empty seat, and there are too many kinds of shoes being offered toward the middle of the circle in twosies. I remember to smile. As I try to smile in a way that's both trustworthy and stern, I orbit the group with my eyes. So this is the cast of our in-house production of *Whose Lie Is It, Anyway?*

I do not judge their faces harshly. Now that I am with them, I get the rather lame sense that we are in this together. Their chins and cheeks appeal more to my sense of let's-get-this-over-with than as a direct challenge of my authority. I don't feel opposed to them at all, really. I feel drawn in.

As I take in each face, I am momentarily inhabited—I become each participant during the flicker of eye contact we share. Without moving my body or features (but within my self-perception) I hold my jaw and my wrists the way they do. I narrow or widen my eyes and raise or lower my chin as my hair grows, shrinks, curls, and balds. It's an inner imitation. A motionless morph. It's an homage—not a lie—because the becoming isn't even a choice.

This loss of bodily boundaries reminds me of when my daughter was just born. I hadn't slept in two days so they took her to the nursery to let me rest. Every time my eyes closed, I became the baby. My mouth wanted and my arms went like second-hands on a watch that has no regard for time. My nose became flattened by my own insistently narrow birth canal. That sensation was my hormones letting me know who was important to the survival of the species. *Don't forget the baby! You are no one, husk. You sleep in minutes now, but the baby sleeps in swaths.*

What could my hormones be up to now, letting me slip into such late-stage shapes? Maybe my perimenopausal estrogen levels are showing me what lies ahead—where I'll soon be putting my shoes in twosies.

That's a misfire, estrogen—we could never afford this place.

I retire my smile and decide to speak before I feel ready, just in case a sudden start shocks me into competency. "Good morning. Thanks for getting the circle started. I'm Candice. I'll be your . . ."

My mouth blanks, but my brain fires a list: *counselor, leader, server, foe, guru, employee, buddy-ol-pal, listener, niece, straight-man, truth diviner.*

Before I land on who I am to them someone else calls out, "Guide."

I nod at him, the orange juice man, and say, "That's right. Thank you."

* * *

I make a big show of pulling up a chair. Instead of picking it up and carrying it, I drag the chair along the floor, so I'm contributing *something* as the incoming hired professional, even if it's only a scraping sound. The people closest to me dramatically scoot their chairs over to make room, which means the people closest to them need to resituate as well. Soon the whole room is loudly scraping their chairs out and back, and the noise reaches such a decibel that I am certain they are mocking me. It's so loud I suspect that half the people are standing in place and grinding the chairs into the floor just to contribute to the ruckus.

When I sit the scraping stops. The shape we've made is still technically round but has become jaggedy like a fried egg. This could be to my advantage—broken chains can't conspire without considerable effort. "Why don't we start with introductions?"

The woman next to me says, "We've all known each other for some time." She points to a man across from her. "He's actually my brother-in-law."

"Right. The introductions would be for my benefit, then. Why don't we make it into a game?" No one audibly groans, but I swear I hear several people swallow at me. "Now hear me out—think of this game as a nod to the history of this group. Quinetta told me about your first couple go-rounds—the silence, then the lying. I've taken that as helpful feedback. Your group history has *heavily* influenced the way I'm approaching this whole endeavor. Have any of you ever played 'Two Truths and a Lie'? You'll each tell the group three tidbits about your life. Two will be true . . . or, let's use the word 'valid'—and one will be made-up. Then the rest of us try to guess which tidbit is fiction."

The self-identified sister-in-law asks, "What do we get if we win?"

I start to say, "It's not that kind of a game," but then I remember how it felt to hold her shape—undefined, graspy. She needs a reward. "I could pat you on the head if you'd like?"

She rolls her eyes and sticks out her tongue a tiny bit to show she knows she's being mocked, but I think we both feel as if I had patted her head. My counseling program really underplayed "gentle ribbing" as a therapeutic technique.

"Who wants to go first?" A woman in a denim jumper waves both of her hands like she's trying to stop a full-speed big rig from running over a tricycler. She seems young for the group, not much older than I am. None of them feel much older than me, now that I sit among them. I'd say they range in age from early sixties to mideighties. When

I pictured myself here I thought I'd be among those who felt like grand-parents—at least two generations removed—but I forgot that time has moved me forward as well. People in retirement homes are more like the age of my parents, my first grade teachers, my coolest aunt. They watched a lot of the same commercials I did.

I nod permission to denim jumper and make a mental note of her volunteering. I've always felt that wanting to go first is a cry for help.

"I'm Marla," she says, "and I'd just like you to know that I was the only one here who told the last guy the truth. I *really did* work at a car dealership owned by a second cousin of Robert Altman, and he *really did* talk over me every time I spoke."

I tell Marla that I believe her while deciding her clarifications and physical location both feel misplaced. Group members in the most jagged seats are forced to lean in or out to see her face, and if we are after the truth then we need clear, plain views. "Why don't we move you into the center?" I look around for a hot seat. The piano bench will do.

I pick up the wooden bench and carry it against my rib cage, the flat top resting right under my breasts. *Seat's taken.* Inside the circle, I set the bench down gently, careful not to make a sound. "There. It's more ceremonial this way. Marla?"

Marla has clearly been waiting her whole life for someone to move her to the center of the group, but she plays it cool by not breaking into a full run. She sits on the bench and puts her thumbs under the shoulder straps of her jumper. "As a child my eyes crossed then went back to normal the very next day, and the doctor said it may have been a stress response to seeing my cat Speedy get hit by the mail truck. Two: When my oldest grandson comes to visit, I pretend I'm less recovered from my stroke than I really am so he'll keep his visits brief. I can't hear any more about his fitness routine nor face the sight of his receding hairline. No wonder he's doing so many pull-ups! Number three: I once made love to a stranger in an outdoor plant nursery. He was an employee there, helping me select which type of low-light flower would replace the collection of rustic mailboxes the previous owners had left on the north side of my house. I didn't tell my husband and he never found out and now he's dead. So is that a foible or a freebie?"

Marla looks around the room with her eyebrows raised, but no one ventures a guess. She spoke so quickly, it's possible that they are just now, in the silence, understanding what she said. I give the lag its moment, then say, "Anyone want to guess which was the lie?"

Marla looks a bit rumpled. Something has confused her. She starts to speak but gets cut off by someone calling out, "Dull grandson!"

"No," she says, "that's true. And he was *such* a thoughtful kid. He used to draw spirals, paper after paper covered in spirals. He wouldn't even consider learning to write a 'P' or a '7'—he was devoted to expressing this one shape. We thought he was a genius, but I think he was just lacking imagination. But wait, did I say—"

A man with droopy shoulders raises his voice above hers. "The sex one! I don't buy it. Weren't there other customers? Didn't you care that they might see your butt? And wouldn't you have wanted to *at least* sit across from him in a booth before sleeping with him? I know you better than that! When Mallory moved in next to you, you wouldn't even say 'good day' to her until she'd been here three months. Am I right?"

Marla shakes her head. Her once frenetic movements are now slow and hesitant—as if speaking expended all her certainty. "Sorry, Richard. That happened too. I had just weaned my youngest son, and my hormones were going wild—a relapse into desire. That man in the nursery . . . gentle yet rugged . . . you should have seen the way he held a garden hose. He saw the way I was looking at him and what I meant by it and then . . . we really went at it."

Many of us nod, picturing and accepting this image. I stop nodding when I consider that my head is moving in time with that long-ago humping. "So, the fake one was when your eyes crossed?" I ask, proud of myself for my ability to recall any one of her rapid-fire memories.

Marla puts her head in her hands and her elbows on her knees to support the topple. From inside the curl of her upper body, she says, "Wait." She lifts back up to show her face. "I messed up. It got muddled somehow—what I meant to say isn't what came out. The one about my eyes is real too. I woke up and saw two of everything in my room: lamp lamp, alarm alarm. I went to tell my mom, and she said that maybe my eyes crossed because I woke up too fast. Now, I do chide my grandchildren for their over-anxious parenting, but Mom could have been a bit *more* concerned about my eyes changing direction in my head!"

"You told us three real stories? Didn't you understand the premise of the game?" I try not to sound harsh, but I am irked that she's undermining the legitimacy I have yet to earn.

In her defense, she looks truly apologetic, bordering on stunned. "I had a lie all ready to go, and somehow I told three real things instead."

We're all quiet. Marla keeps straightening her upper body and then lifting her bottom off the bench, but instead of fully standing she sits back down and settles into the curl she'd just left. She does this a couple times, managing to stay and go simultaneously. Maybe Marla wants to move back to her seat and end her turn but feels like she has to stay and be punished for how her turn turned out.

Finally the sister-in-law says, "It's okay, Marla. Could have happened to anyone." Since the sister-in-law pointed out a flaw in my logic before even telling me her name, I get the sense that she's offering Marla this kindness for a reason other than radical empathy. Maybe Marla has memory problems and often gets confused? Oh wow . . . I had not considered anything like that. Oh wow . . . I am *wildly* unequipped for this job.

I add, "Yes, no big deal, Marla. Thanks for sharing." Marla completes her standing sequence, and as I watch her return to relative obscurity, my eye catches a tree branch out the window, moving in the wind. I want to go cradle the branch for offering me a touchstone for the world outside this group. *Oh, yes, everything else.* Leaves, shingles, road signs, the box store across the street where all the purchases beep beep beep. My car, waiting for me. Gum on the sidewalk. Beloved pets. Unwanted children. My own daughter, at school on a coast I've never visited. My ex-husband, who the fuck cares. My sister, tapping her toe. Quinetta, at a desk, reworking the budget. Or Quinetta, listening outside this door.

I refocus on the circle. The man to Marla's left has moved to the
bench. While I zoned out, the group wordlessly decided we would
travel clockwise. He starts talking, and I make a mental note that he's
not the kind of person who waits for a "go-ahead."

"My aunt used to come to my baseball games and call me 'Lug Nut'
while I was at bat. Like she'd yell, 'Let's go, Lug Nut,' and all the other
guys on the team would laugh and joke about my nuts being long
and heavy. I couldn't tell them she'd used that pet name since I was a
baby because being babyish was worse than having bulky balls, and I
couldn't ask my aunt to stop calling me that without acknowledging
the existence of my increasingly demanding private body parts and also
hurting her feelings. So I quit baseball and took up smoking. Item two:
My first wife wouldn't let me smoke indoors. Item three: I was once
fired from a factory job for getting into an altercation with a mechani-
cal arm, but it was *complete* bullshit because it was my first offense and
because I told them they could take the money out of my paycheck
to repair the damages. Nowadays we aren't surprised when someone
takes a machine's side in an argument, but back then it really stung."

He's turned slightly red while telling this factory story, a real rile, so
it must be true. Before I can rule out one of the remaining tidbits, the
sister-in-law says, "Your items were just a list of grievances, Thomas."

Thomas shrugs. I tell my own shoulders to be still, to let Thomas
have his own shrug.

Marla calls out, "I remember what my lie was going to be! I was
going to tell you that I went on *Wheel of Fortune* in the early nine-
ties, and when I went to spin the wheel it caught the tip of my acrylic
fingernail, and a little piece of nail broke off my finger, flew into the
air, and landed in another contestant's eye. And I was going to say
the woman with my fingernail in her eye went on to win the game—
including the wowza prize at the end—all with one eye squinted shut.
And everyone treated her like *such* a hero, even though I was the one
sporting a disgraced manicure on national television. I thought that
was a pretty good lie for such short notice—show business, a rivalry,

plus a comment on the ridiculousness of vanity. I've never had a mani-cure in my life, though, so you all might have smelled a rat. Anyway, when I was talking earlier it was like the lie flew away, but now that I'm back in my seat I've got a hold of it."

Thomas is looking at Marla like he's got a new grievance. I thank Marla for the footnote and ask her to respond to what Thomas has shared.

"Oh. Right. I'm gonna say . . . the baseball thing with the dirty nick-name. Is that fake?"

Thomas shakes his head. "Nope. Although it's not an entirely untrue nickname at this point." He smiles, then looks baffled, like whatever has just occurred to him would have overshadowed and prevented the smile had it occurred seconds earlier.

Marla takes another guess. "It must be the bit about smoking, then, because you seemed pretty pissed about that robot."

Thomas rubs his cheeks in a manner usually reserved for those with beards. He must be around eighty, so even though he's clean-shaven now, it's quite possible that he has spent more time sporting facial hair than I've spent time sporting a heartbeat. He says, "Those are both true."

The group reacts—the sharp intake of breath, the low grumble of disbelief. The reaction comes too fast and too neat, like they counted off beforehand—deciding the ones would suck air and the twos would go, "What the hell?" I'd been annoyed with Marla, but now I feel a rising anger, a direct challenge, a group effort against me. I'd been warned but not until the last minute. There hadn't been enough time to get my hackles up to a height that could have foreseen this. I ask, "You told us three real things too?"

Thomas looks very *poor Thomas*. "I really didn't mean to. It's like once my mouth started going the lie refused to come out. I don't understand it myself."

Marla jumps back in. "Yes, that's how I felt *exactly*! The lie became lodged, and it stayed that way until I got back to my seat."

Thomas stands up from the hot seat. "I once called into a radio station that was giving away tickets to see the Four Tops. The forty-fourth caller would be the winner—that's what they said, over and over, probably twice a minute. I was number forty-four, and yet they refused to give me the prize because I couldn't remember their call letters, which I thought was silly and spiteful. I knew their phone number, and that's what mattered. I'll never forgive WEPS, although after that incident their tagline felt more apt. WEPS: We hits you where it hurts." Thomas nods a bit like he's settled something and then points to the seat below him. "It's the bench. That was my lie, just now. While I was on the bench it couldn't come out, and when I stood up, there it was, easy. The bench won't let us lie."

As I say, "Oh, come on," Marla gasps. "Oh my god. That has to be it!"

Right away, first instinct, I feel resigned to playing the fool. I'll let them play-act whatever they want, fine, who cares, think of all the preventive healthcare I can get with this insurance. And then, disregarding all pap smears and cancer screenings, I immediately override my own decision. If they'd been more subtle about their trickery, maybe I could have let it slide, but the gall of a persuasive bench gag was *too much*, even for my newborn hackles. I'm a liar, not a chump.

"You two expect me to believe the piano bench has some sort of truth serum effect, and you expect me to believe this *even though* I know that you all messed with both of your previous counselors?"

Marla nods. "It looks bad, I agree. But when would we have been able to plan this? We didn't know you'd choose this game, and we couldn't have predicted that there would be a piano bench, much less a piano bench with this kind of power and integrity. And remember, I didn't participate in those other shenanigans! I'm above shenanigans. This whole deal is above shenanigans! What if the bench is made from the wood of an old confessional booth?"

Thomas clears his throat. "Not God . . . could be a . . . one of those . . . sugar pill . . . placebo effects . . . an effect, though, *definitely*." He's still standing above the bench as he offers this fragmented theory.

I look around at the others, trying to gauge whether they seem skeptical or implicated. The sister-in-law is right beside me. Her profile reveals nothing. I try to remember what it felt like to hold her undefined, graspy shape. I slip into her shape again to see if there's any change, if the shape feels up to anything, but it feels the same as before—no more defined, no less deprived.

I glance at the branch and tell them that if they want to pretend the bench is magic and sends special messages through their butts, up their spines, and right into their sense of right-and-wrong then they are free to do so. "But," I say, "I want you to know that my allowing it is not the same as my falling for it."

The sister-in-law leans over to say, "I'm on your side, just so you know. I was a middle grade science teacher, and Newton didn't have a Law of Woo-Woo. I think Marla got confused by her own enthusiasm, and then Thomas worked himself into a tizzy with his grievances. Ask Ellory to go. She's a tough cookie, not one for groupthink." She points to a woman who must be the most senior member of the circle. Ellory is sitting cross-legged in bold colors. Her nails are painted a dismal red, and I interpret her expression as *how-did-it-come-to-this?*

"Ellory," I ask, "do you want to go next?"

She eyes the person next to Thomas's empty seat, the rightful heir to the turn. "I could go at any point." She speaks evenly, giving each word equal weight. People who'd spent less time on earth would want to emphasize *I* or *any*.

"Would you mind?" *My neighbor here says you aren't prone to bench-related hysteria.*

Ellory stands, revealing her outfit to be a full and true glory. Her blouse is brash-red with a black-and-white cross-hatch pattern at the collar, around the breast pocket, and at the wrists, where identical bracelets bear the same two collar colors, remixed into checkered squares. Her white hair has been curled and then seemingly finger-twisted into points.

Thomas passes Ellory on the way to his seat. I want to see him bow to her.

It's apparent that walking causes her some slight pain, but her movements also display poise and a lack of hesitancy. She must be in fairly good health. If she required a higher level of care she wouldn't live in an independent living facility.

Ellory sits down on the bench and recrosses her legs. Her spine is held straight, a habit that has surely helped keep her out of assisted living. She looks right at me and says, "The problem is that people aren't willing to believe facts that don't fit into their narrative. So their truths shift and recalibrate, and some fall away completely, becoming events that never happened."

"What the hell is that supposed to mean? Are you calling me a . . . what are you calling me?" This is from Thomas, causing me to doubt he ever had the forbearance necessary to grow a full beard.

"I was not speaking directly to you or about you, Thomas. It must be tiring to hear every statement as a challenge. You must be exhausted. What I meant is that people—including but not limited to Thomas— only keep hold of the facts that align with the visions of themselves and of this life to which they already subscribe."

Marla calls out, "Are you saying that the bench has no influence?"

Ellory repositions both her bracelets, which tend to slide toward her elbows when she gesticulates. "I have nothing to say about the bench."

I should jump in here and do some guiding. "Could you give us an example, Ellory? I'm sure everyone would like to better understand you."

"Maybe so. Or maybe they don't want to understand anything other than what they've already deemed understood."

Sister-in-law leans over again to whisper, "I should have mentioned about Ellory—the reason she's not one for groupthink is because the group can't comprehend what the hell she's thinking."

Ellory continues, "Did you notice that even Thomas's fake story was about getting screwed over? And Marla's lie was about being given the wrong attention from the right people or the right attention from the wrong people, just like with her grandson and the nursery employee and her mother's response to her eye problem."

"Maybe you're right about . . . whatever you're saying. But why couldn't we say them while we were on the bench, Ellory? Explain that." Marla says this, but Thomas nods to indicate that he's saying it too.

Ellory touches one of her hair tips. "I have nothing to say about the bench."

"Do you want to tell us your three items, then, Ellory?" I admire Ellory's backbone and outfit, but I'm starting to feel nostalgic for the bumbling, inconsistent contestants of yesterminutes.

"Sure, I can tell you three things. But keep in mind that they've all been run through my internal signal-scrambler, so while I believe I'm giving two truths and a lie, a different signal-scrambler might call them two never-evers and an absolutely."

"We will keep that in mind, Ellory." As I validate Ellory, I consider all the vices I've given up in pursuit of a longer life—beer, cigarettes, Sweet'n Low, Timmy Wayne Trexler, tanning booths, breakfast foods that keep my lips glazed until 11:00. I might take those up again. Living long enough to master a listen-here tone while simultaneously living long enough to understand and detest the underpinnings of society does not appeal to me. I don't want to start talking back to the TV.

Ellory stares at the floor but gives the impression that she'll start at any moment. Perhaps this is what it looks like to consult your signal-scrambler. She looks up and speaks in her now-famous even meter.

"As a girl I would squeeze my kneecaps at all times because I thought it made my legs look more attractive and shapely. At recess I abstained from tag since my stiff legs couldn't move fast enough to get away from nor catch the others. Instead I stood along the fence hoping someone would notice how nice my legs looked. Moving on . . ." Ellory pauses here to look marginally alarmed. Her eyes and her mouth go pancake— soft and round. Is she pantomiming alarm? Is she truly fighting against the bench's powers, trying to overcome its will?

She recovers and smiles. "In the early 1960s my husband and I were invited to a dinner party at the home of one of his senior colleagues. After the meal, I found myself alone in the kitchen with the colleague's wife. The table conversation had been excruciating—strained, overly formal, and boring to the point that I felt relief when a knife scraped against a plate. But in the kitchen, life felt back on. The hostess had turned on the radio and was swaying a bit as she carried dishes to the sink. The opened window let in night air and a sense of renewal. I was leaning on the counter, nibbling on pepperjack squares, when she bent over to scrape leftovers down the garbage disposal; I don't know what came over me, but I reached out and pinched her ass cheek. She didn't react at all, so there was no space for me to apologize or explain, and the next thing I knew we were back at the table eating lemon meringue pie. Without a reaction, I began to seriously doubt that I existed at all, and yet the pie on my plate was getting smaller and smaller and had to be going somewhere, down into *something*."

That story took it out of Ellory, like maybe it was *too* true. Her spine has exhaled, causing her shoulders to settle closer to a stoop. Ellory seems to be catching her breath, or settling some other internal score. She's let her bracelets wander.

"The last of my three is this: Everyone has a great wound." She emphasizes each word, so they hit hard while remaining even. *Everyone. Has. A. Great. Wound.*

The sister-in-law turns to me. "Does that last one count? It's a little broad." Before I respond, she takes her concerns to Ellory. "That one isn't even about you."

Ellory doesn't blink. "I am included in the everyone."

Thomas asks why, then, didn't she offer up her own personal wound.

"As part of a game? In the middle of a circle? On a piano bench? When everyone I love is dead?"

I need to reinsert myself—whether real or artificial, this thing's growing out beyond the circle we've made. "It's okay Ellory. You don't have to justify or defend your choices. So, we know the great wound is true. Is the pinching story true?"

Ellory brings her arms in close to her upper body, one crossing her chest and the other under her chin. She nods, yes, bumping her knuckles.

"And," I continue, "was the knee story true?"

She nods slower but still yes.

The sister-in-law leans over to say, "Well, that's my bad. I assumed Ellory would rise above." She pats my knee. "If it's any consolation, we *all* have a great wound."

Ellory quickly stands as if to say, *"I have nothing to say about the bench"* one last time before returning to her seat. Her movements are still poised, though I cannot tell if she's shaken up and defeated or brazen, exiting stage left.

I stare at the branch out the window the whole time I move from my seat to the bench. The branch is not duplicitous, requires no decoding. It is a branch. I will not deliberate.

"Hello, my name is Candice, and these are my three things. My father spent his night hours in our tornado shelter. The shelter was a grassy mound with a door, out behind the house. We were not to disturb him. If we needed our father after dinnertime, we were to go to Mother, who would descend down into the earth to let him know he was invited to our card game. After he died, I went down into the tornado shelter. He could no longer be disturbed there. He was below different ground. I took an oil burning lantern and didn't know what to hope for. If I found only benign and boring items, why did he choose them over me? If I found anything illicit, then I'd be disturbed in addition to grieving. I found a toolbox with a hammer but no nails, screws but no screwdriver. I found several crime novels in paperback. I thumbed through them and found that my father had underlined the characters' names. There was a ruler, bullets, a coffee mug, and several cans of kidney beans. A plastic crate held rags, aerosol sprays, and a wrestling trophy that did not bear my father's name. I realized I was looking for a letter with my name and that I was not going to find it. When I went back into the daylight, I brought a can of beans with me and read the label as if it were addressed to me. *Dear Candice. Store any unused portion in a separate container. Love, Daddy.*"

I had meant to deliver a short, punchy anecdote . . . one that showed how clever and resourceful I can be . . . preferably one that didn't end on sad beans. Maybe I'm not in control of what I share. Maybe I'm not even in control of what I believe. The bench has become a seat-powered Ouija board. *Was that you? Was that me? Or are we under the jurisdiction of the Law of Woo-Woo?*

I burrow deep into what I mean to say before resuming. I'll inhabit myself, thank you.

"Everyone has a *great* wound." That was not entirely what I intended, but it seems that I have complete control over where I put my emphasis. "I personally have a *truly* outstanding wound."

The participants, those I am meant to guide, appear to be leaning in for my final statement. Are they closing in rapt or hungry? Are they on my side? Is my side the one for truth? Is my side in favor of self-protection? Of guard dogs? Is Quinetta outside the door holding the golden rule or a balance scale or a finish line? Does the branch resent being blown? Is my car still outside? Does the piano miss its bench?

I will tell a lie next, I know I can do it. If I can speak a string of untrue words, then I'm proven both right and mighty. And my ability to lie will mean that *they* lied, but I've already forgiven them because I so recently held their shapes, because I am so, so rapidly becoming their shapes. I love them for their lying. Right now their lies are my very favorite thing about them.

But if the false words I want to say are instead replaced by a verbal glimpse into my great wound, then I won't be able to love anyone here. My love only goes where I tell it, and I send it toward control and order, doled out neatly when I have the time, when I'm up for it, when it's safe to come out. My love sidesteps the limitless.

"I got pregnant . . . in . . . Aunt Renatta's . . ."

The Buick LeSabre and the Lincoln Town Car both rev in my mouth and all through me, but I don't know if either car is fast enough to break the boundaries I've tried so hard to keep.

These New Francescas

I had been dating Brandon for about four months when he stepped back from tending to his own kids and let me take over the brunt of the childcare. Before this baton-passing moment, he performed his parenting for me like a form of wooing. When he refilled his son's glass of milk, he bent from the waist and poured slowly, making sure I was watching. When his daughter banged her shin on the coffee table and ran to be consoled, he patted her back but looked into *my* eyes when he said, "Are you okay? Did that table hurt you?"

I thought he did this to highlight his sensitive, nurturing side—showing me the skills he would use in our partnership. *See how I could care for you.* But it turns out the performances were more of an apprenticeship than a mating dance. *Pat her back like this—pat pat pat. Not a flat palm, a slight cupping. Pour the glass two-thirds full of milk. Pay attention so I can stop paying attention.*

Brandon had Danny, Alexandra, and Rhea every other weekend. When we didn't have the kids, we functioned as a childfree couple—staying out late, wearing underwear in hallways, shouting obscenities at our phones. But when the kids came over, he morphed into his papa-performance-mode. He wore flannel pajama pants, became slightly befuddled and prone to muttering, and would turn in by 10:30. I enjoyed it, really—it was like dating the star of a stage play and getting to sleep in his private dressing room.

Then one weekend, without formally announcing his retirement, he slumped back and made helpless eyes at me whenever the children needed anything. The first instance was when Rhea misplaced her sweater. After looking in the immediate vicinity of her body, she deemed it "totally nowhere." Brandon made no move toward the coat closet, nor the hooks in her bedroom. He didn't bend over to see if she'd left it balled up under the love seat. Instead, he hooked his elbow over the back of his chair, to show how committed he was to not getting up, and said, "Maybe Miss Melinda could help you?" in the gently suggestive tone that doctors use as they put you under anesthesia. *Go down easy, let this take you, let your will fall out of my way.*

I should have said, *Does my agreeing to find this sweater free you from all of your parental obligations henceforth? And second of all, don't call me Miss Melinda because she sounds like the lone human on a children's show otherwise populated by puppets.* But instead of saying anything, I walked into the living room, picked up Rhea's sweater from the arm of the couch, and handed it to her.

Brandon made a big show of the gesture, as if I'd pulled the child from a well. "Wasn't it incredibly kind of Miss Melinda to get you your sweater?" *Didn't she move swiftly? Has anyone ever picked up a sweater with such verve? Doesn't she love doing for others, and isn't that ultimately her purpose and her calling? Don't you think she'd like to make us dinner, possibly enchiladas?*

Here's why I didn't huff or balk or leave: I *did* like the feeling of having warmed Rhea's little shoulders. When she thanked me, she dipped her head toward her shoulder, and her brown curls fell over her face, which hid the fact that she looked just like her mother, and I wanted to pull her to me and say idiotic things like, *Everything happens for a reason. When a door closes there's some corresponding deal with a window. Time and wounds are on the same track, sweet girl. Take it from me, take all of it.*

I have a caretaking instinct—I can't help it. As a girl I had at least nine baby dolls, all named Francesca. I'd bring the Francescas with me when I bathed. If I left them on my bed, I could feel how much they missed me, and I was completely unable to enjoy my bubbles.

Perhaps Brandon was banking on my having this instinct, which was socialized right into me. I'm sure some of it was inborn and then bolstered by certain hormones, but the point is that I didn't install this instinct *myself*. I didn't choose it.

This duty shift was nearly a year ago. Time blurs, contracts, and rushes when you're taking care. Now Brandon needs taking care of too, even when we don't have the kids. He's forgotten how to do laundry or sweep the entryway, how to put cheese inside a tortilla and melt it in the microwave.

I'd be lying if I said it didn't feel holy and tidy to stuff my own needs down to make room for his, for theirs. I'm *Miss Melinda*, after all. Watch me do what you've asked. Look how I hold my shoulders without a hint of hunching resentment. See how I no longer have the energy to worry about my job, my savings account, my thyroid, my friend from college who reached out for help and never received my response, my check engine light.

Today we're picking up the kids and taking them to the mall for roast beef sandwiches and quilted vests, then to the art museum for a children's craft. Brandon is in what I call "drive mode," which serves as his transitional state between semi-attentive boyfriend and underperforming co-parent. Earlier, after easy morning-breath sex, he replaced the sheets on the bed totally unprompted. He kissed the back of my neck as I locked the door. Now, driving, he's a different Brandon. He's wearing mirrored sunglasses and looks like he's mad at the steering wheel. I'm attracted to his anger and determination—he'd use these to protect me if I happened to be standing right behind him.

Brandon pulls the van up to the house he purchased with his ex-wife. It's a two-story Victorian with white siding and a wrap-around porch. I always try to picture him mowing this lawn, cleaning these gutters, touching that wife. When he honks the horn, I jump.

"Honking is rude. Why don't you knock on the door?"

"Making us wait is rude. If you want knocking, then go do it yourself. Knock yourself out." He laughs at his joke. I see myself in his glasses, and I do not look amused. Miss Melinda looks tired.

Before I can decide to go to the door, the children come running out with their weekend bags. She's let Danny leave the house in shorts. I check the dash. It's forty-six degrees. Danny should wear pants unless it hits sixty or he's playing indoor sports. I don't know how she could make a child and then send him out into the world with exposed shins. Now I'll be worried about his legs all over the mall—top floor, bottom level, food court, escalator, fountain—and in the museum, too, surrounded by all manner of giant gold frames.

There's a sibling tussle over who will sit where—elbows are invoked, as well as the term "buttwad." Brandon looks straight ahead through the windshield at where he wants to take us, so I turn around to end the argument by giving them seating assignments. I put Danny closest to the front, so he can feel the car's heat on his legs. Brandon asks if we are ready to go, even though he's already pulled away from the house, even though he's nearly to the corner, even though his children have yet to click their buckles.

After finishing the roast beef and the two-inch pile of napkins, we tackle the mall in two groups. I take the girls vest shopping in stores that play pop anthems and honor online coupons, while Brandon takes Danny to the outdoor store, where he can get a vest with meaningful pockets in a print devoid of personal expression. The vests are for the professional family photo I have scheduled for tomorrow. I'm not going to be in the picture since I am not an official family member, but I'd like it to be nice enough to hang above the sofa I vacuum weekly.

Alexandra and Rhea fall in love with the first sequined sweaters they see, the kind that change color when you pet them like a cat.

"It's not a sweater photo," I tell them. "I signed up for the 'vests on a bench' package. The photographer *did* offer a sweater package, but that would involve all four of you climbing into a clawfoot tub in the backyard."

In the end, I buy them the sweaters *and* the vests. Layers for my girls. After I pay, I sit them down in the chairs outside the dressing room and redo their hair using the brush I keep in my purse. If they'd stuck to trying on vests, their hair wouldn't have gotten mussed.

Back in the van, Danny holds up his purchase. It's camouflage with gaping pockets at the bottom and strappy suspenders at the top. "It's a turkey vest!"

I look at Brandon. "You bought him a hunting vest for the family photo?"

He puts on his sunglasses. "It turns into a seat! Show her, Danny."

Danny unbuckles the vest's strap and pulls down on a piece of fabric. "For sitting in the woods!"

"But you don't hunt. You don't even like to play tag."

He shrugs. "It was the coolest one."

I reach behind my seat and pat his shin. "I'm sure it was, Danny."

At the art museum, the craft of the week is "toothpick candelabras." A large gallery room houses rows of tables offering marshmallows, toothpicks, and laminated pictures of candelabras to inspire the mini-artists. The children sit down and hand me their coats, which I hold on my lap like I am pregnant with their outer layers.

Alexandra, being the oldest, gets to work on her design without any need for approval or guidance. "I'm going to make a five-armed candelabra with a coiled base."

As Alexandra works up a rough sketch of her design, I ask Danny and Rhea to please stop eating marshmallows by the fistful. "It's about context," I tell them. "In a home, marshmallows are food, but in a craft setting they are supplies. They are possibilities."

Rhea spits her wad of marshmallow goo onto the table. When she registers my disapproval, she sticks a toothpick into the wad. "One arm!"

Brandon asks Danny what he's going to make, pointing out the impressive creation of a child sitting behind us and telling him, "You can top that."

Danny grabs a few toothpicks, eager to capitalize on this opportunity for paternal praise. He attaches two sticks together using a marshmallow, and his father says, "What are you doing? Poke them on farther. Tighter. You don't want it to be flimsy."

I'm considering the most effective way to distract Brandon from continuing this kind of pestering and belittling when Rhea says, "Miss Melinda?"

I suppose she's calling her spitty one-pronged effort good enough because she is paying no attention to the craft at hand. Instead she's standing up, taking in the massive paintings that surround the tables.

She points to one. "Who is that?"

The painting is of a nude woman in a small fishing boat. She is reaching over the side of the boat to reel what she's hooked—a golden fish with breasts and a tongue. The fisherwoman is wide-eyed about her catch, perhaps because it's not the meal she had in mind. Her stomach, in side-view, is an open wound—blood, organs, and eyeballs. She has one leg up on the boat's edge to brace herself against the fish's bosomy strength. Her toenails, curled over the rim, are painted red. I don't like the way she's pulling and bracing at the same time, how hungry she looks, how resigned. I don't like how I relate to the image against my will.

"And why is she naked?" Rhea asks. She doesn't ask why the woman's organs are on display.

"How about you keep working on your candelabra?" I gesture at her wad. "That thing won't be giving off much light."

Rhea ignores my critique and asks about the painting to the right of the naked fisher. It's of six children, wearing cut-off jean shorts, crouching in a circle to dig in the dirt with sticks. The children are all endeavoring toward the creation of one big hole. In the background, a panther watches them from a tree, and a mother watches from a porch. Under the ground, we see the pile of red bones they are getting closer and closer to unearthing.

Rhea wants to know what it means.

"I don't know, honey. I think it has something to do with wanting. Or danger. Art is open to interpretation."

She stares at the painting of the children and their efforts. "I think it's about missing your mother."

I exhale too quickly and lose my grip on the coats in my lap. One of them falls to the floor. I pick it up. I apologize. No one is listening.

Brandon has completely taken over Danny's project—diligently making the candelabra himself, wearing his sunglasses on top of his head. Danny has gone back to eating marshmallows. Probably for warmth. Alexandra, having created exactly what she intended to create, is working on a second candelabra inspired by the gothic example on the sheet in front of her.

Rhea has a toothpick in her mouth. She's tipping it up and down with her teeth, like a snake using its tongue to perceive new surroundings. "Miss Melinda, is that a painting of God?"

She's pointing behind me. A rogue curl has fallen over her eye. I love all of her, even the part of her that will never miss me.

I don't look back. I say, "Yes."

Perceptor Weekly

The school lunch menu has once again landed in the *Herald*'s inbox with the subject line LUNCH MENU and an attached document titled *LUNCH MENU TEMPLATE*. This email comes every Wednesday afternoon, sent by the school secretary. I find comfort in how little it varies. If there's pizza, there's corn. Hamburgers mean tots. Each combo served with diced fruit. Always "choice of milk."

We print the menu in the newspaper every week, even though the whole month's menu is available online at every moment. This town runs on habit. *Put school menu in the upper-right corner on page 4. Send this into the* Herald *on Wednesday. Scoop corn into the slot beside the pizza.*

But I won't bash habit. I appreciate the weekly rituals—the way they carry on the same—even more since Tony showed up. I look up from my computer to see about him. When you remember Tony, you immediately look at him to see what he's doing at that moment, but then you look and he seems so ordinary. Sitting and typing.

Well, *bearing down* more than sitting. You can't tell by looking, but he's a paperweight in human form. His average-sized body is much heavier than most. By hundreds of pounds. He walks like the Tin Man during a blizzard. We can't find chairs strong enough.

I don't know why they made him like this if he's supposed to be inconspicuous. It's possible that his density helps with his process. Maybe his true body was shoved into this ill-fitting meat puppet. Maybe the weight is full of sensors and hearing mechanisms. I'm not privy to the process. The terms prohibit me from asking too many questions.

He's typing and scrolling. I'll say this: he's an excellent proofreader. I run it all by him now, even the captions. He knows all the faces in town, so if we mix up the names of two boys under the photo of the seventh grade basketball team, he catches it, easy. He instinctively zones in on anything untrue. It's helpful. It's unnerving.

There's a ribbon-cutting ceremony starting soon, a new chain restaurant opening down the street in the building that used to be a pawn shop. Most of the buildings in town have been pawn shops at one point, so that's not really a good way to differentiate buildings. This one happens to be on the corner. This one is painted brown. I need to send a photographer down there so we have enough happy-good-news items this week. I could send Trish or Deena. Tony can't walk that far, and I'm not allowed to send him out of the office, anyway. Per terms, his newspaper contributions are all of the indoor variety. Maybe I'll go myself. I could use the sunshine and the break from sitting.

I pop my head into the main room (in a bigger operation it might be called the newsroom) and tell the girls I'm going out to take a photo. I put my camera around my neck and walk past Tony at the front desk. I don't need to tell him what I'm doing. He already knows. As soon as I thought about the photo, the pawn shops, the sunshine, it all was tabulated somewhere in his concrete poundage. I wave anyway, to contribute to my own feelings of normalcy.

The new restaurant is only a few buildings away. It will serve pitas. You can choose what you want in your pita, insofar as what you want in your pita is what they've laid out in front of you. There's a man and a woman standing behind the red ribbon. The man is from the bank. The woman, I assume, is the person bringing pita to our fair town. I don't recognize her, so she must have moved here to start this business. I know everyone—the town is very small, and I run the newspaper.

There's not much of a crowd here to watch the ribbon cutting. There're a couple kids who must belong to the pita woman because she keeps looking down at them with eyes that say *don't even*. The owners of the neighboring businesses have come out. That woman owns the diner, technically a competitor for food dollars. That man owns the pawn shop, the one with the bike in the window. Always a bike. And me. I am here to provide the event an audience, but later, reading about it in their own homes.

Now that I'm here, they can start the ceremonial snip. The bank man welcomes us, says something about keeping local dollars local. The woman talks about her vision for fast, healthy meals wrapped up in whole wheat—a prepackaged vision she paid for with a franchise fee. I take some notes on my phone to write this up later. *Local dollars. Whole wheat wraps.* The pawn shop owner instigates an applause, and we all clap along so we can then leave. I stop the pita woman to confirm her name and the details for the grand opening. Kids will eat free, drinks not included.

I think of Tony perceiving all this. Will he wonder why we went outside to watch a string be cut in two? Will he understand the symbolism? Will his report to whomever convey a sense of community and perseverance? Will he understand why the drinks aren't included?

I resent being forced to see us all from above, a removed perspective. At first it was fun. An audience—let's put on a show! Tell them about Christmas trees! Show them how we swim in lakes, float on our backs! Ballet! Childbirth! Ooh, ooh, pineapple upside down cakes, the part where you turn it over onto a serving plate! Show them that! But there was no feedback. No applause. Just tabulations. Just perception, ongoing and without comment.

I shouldn't have been surprised. When Tony showed up, he said, "I am a Perceptor." He didn't say, "Here we are, now entertain us."

When he first came to the office, he asked to speak to me privately about a job. I told him we had no openings. He said, "Be that as it may . . . ," which I'd never heard anyone utter in real life. He was insistent on a private meeting. I would have been frightened, him being such a forward and unknown man, but his tone had no hint of malice. I now know (from the chatty yet matter-of-fact tidbits that Tony drops) that his voice was engineered to put humans at ease so that he could more easily perceive them. I led him to my office. He stood, knowing the plastic visitor chair would not hold. I remained standing also.

"How can I help you?"

"I am a Perceptor. I realize you don't know what that means, so I will tell you. I'm here to make reports on your town."

"We aren't looking for a reporter at this time, but I can keep your résumé . . ."

"Please sit."

I don't know why I sat. It was my office. From my seated position, I watched him move his hand to his hip. The effort it took—it was like his arm was filled with something other than bone and muscle. I pictured sand or water inside his arm, then a smattering of beach umbrellas. I hadn't had a vacation in a decade.

"I am a Perceptor. I realize you don't know what that means, so I will tell you. I'm here to make reports on your town. I have to be close enough to the townspeople to perceive them. I report their thoughts and actions. I report their inputs and outputs. I cause no harm. They feel nothing. In fact, they feel a slight temporary warmth in their temporal lobe that they will probably mistake for happiness."

I thought of who I could call to get this man some help. My husband's friend Andy drives an ambulance. Deena volunteered for a suicide hotline in college. I decided that playing along, taking him seriously, would be best for my safety in that moment.

"Where . . . do these reports go?"

"My response to that question is this: I am not from a governmental agency. I am not affiliated with any religious body. I am supposed to tell you that I am something akin to a cosmic fact-checker."

I laughed and then understood I wasn't supposed to laugh, even though his face didn't change. It was the lack of change that conveyed it. I now know that my laugh was documented so that other Perceptors could avoid the pitfalls of having their spiel mistaken for a joke.

I tried to look like I hadn't laughed. I picked up a pen.

He said, "You will be compensated. We are aware of the hard times facing print newspapers. There will be sizable monthly payments. I will also offer my services to your newspaper free of charge. Perceptors are being placed at newspapers all over the world at this moment. You will be part of a big operation. We know you place value on feeling part of something bigger than yourselves. In some countries, we are working as drivers or fruit sellers. I am telling you that as a bonus tidbit. I am not expressly told to offer you this level of detail."

Once the subject of money was introduced, I was pretty sure the whole thing was a scam. He would ask for my banking information next. Instead he reached into his pocket and pulled out a sweaty piece of paper. He laid it on my desk. A check written out to the *Ashton Weekly Herald* for $2,500.

"Your first payment."

I picked it up. The signature read PSA. I wasn't aware of a scam that paid out money. I owed the printing press $1,800. Our computers were from 2015.

I said, "I'm still not sure what you're asking here."

"Everyone will say that. It's very hard for you to understand. Take comfort in the fact that your understanding is not needed. We only ask for compliance. I am going to need steel chairs. Purchase several."

He opened my door and went to the desk at the front of the office. Slowly. He could barely move his body. The word "lumbering" doesn't suffice. Perhaps the phrase "reanimated corpse filled to the scalp with asphalt" does. The floor creaked but held.

"I will use this desk."

"That's Trish's desk."

"Trish takes pain pills recreationally and has sexual fantasies about a man in a movie about war. She collects silver baby spoons. She has one engraved with the word *Gertie*, which we believe is the name of the baby it once fed."

"How do you know that?"

"I am a Perceptor. It will take seven full explanations and three specific examples of my skills before you understand. That is an average. It will likely take less time for you because your intelligence is high and your responsiveness to new ideas is moderate."

This was amusing, at least, now that I'd decided he wasn't a threat. And since he'd given me money.

"Go ahead and hit me with more specific examples then. Let's get that out of the way."

"Your kids are twelve and fifteen, and they talk to you 30 percent less than they did at age five. Their bodies touch your body 82 percent less often than they did at age three. You live in a house with eight rooms. You married at age twenty. You wish your husband were smarter, and when he chews with his mouth open your sexual desire reaches an all-time low. Your father looks out his window every time a car drives by."

I could not respond. My father, he's always expecting some package.

He said, "You will need to be alone for some time now. Please order the chairs. And I will need a private room for Sending. It is suggested that many newspapers still have darkrooms. Such rooms work nicely for our purposes."

He slo-mo ushered me back into my office and closed me in. I could hear him up front, going through the drawers, typing on the password-protected computer, shuffling papers. A woman came in to place an ad. She was selling a deep freeze. He knew the protocol, charged the right amount based on word count. He put the cash in the drawer. He was good with the customer, warm and helpful. Our shopkeeper bell rang when she opened the door to leave, and Tony cried out "DING" at the exact same time.

* * *

It's Thursday, the day the paper is released. Trish has picked up the bundled copies from the press, and we have three hours to assemble, address, tie, and bag the papers and get them to the post office. Sandy down at the P.O. cuts us no slack on the mail cut-off. If it's 6:02 she'll just shake her head at us when we pull up to the back dock. I hope Tony is letting someone know about this so she's marked down as a harsh bitch, cosmically.

It's all hands on deck for mailing papers. Even Tony helps, seated at a small fold-out table and affixing pre-printed mailing labels on each paper. Most of our papers will be delivered within a five-mile radius, but we have a handful of out-of-state subscribers. A seemingly well-to-do couple from Toronto found one of our old issues in an antique suitcase they bought on EBay and called up asking for a subscription. I assume they find our news to be quaint. I assume they read aloud to each other, that they point and laugh. *On Sunday there's a pancake breakfast to raise money for the fire department. Look at the mayor's hair, do you think he graduated high school? The Methodist church is selling potted plants. These homecoming queen candidates look like dented cans. I hope this homely girl with her eyes closed wins. Her bangs alone deserve a crown.*

First, we assemble the papers by stuffing them together. The paper is printed in two sections, so the second half of the paper is slid inside the first to make a full issue. Our weekly shopper goes inside each paper. And the paid advertising inserts must be put in too. This week our inserts are a thin, slick ad for Pita Way (impossible to pick up) and a small postcard-like ad for a national window company.

The process is this: Arrange your paper stacks with the innermost innards on your right. Stick your fingertips into the communal finger-goop. The goop makes it easier to pick up one paper at a time, so you can be swift-of-arm. Pick up window postcard, put it on top of slick Pita, pick up both of those, put them on top of shopper, pick up all three, slide them into the B section of the paper, then slide the stuffed B into the A, and that's one paper done. Repeat until your fingers are totally black.

Trish, Deena, and I stand and work at one massively long concrete table. It's an astonishing table; it comes up to our breasts. Maybe there's a better word for it than "table" (industrial slab?), but it has both a surface and legs. The top is thick glossy concrete held up by green wooden legs the size of small trees.

Stuffing is mindless work (all in the wrists), so we are able to talk as we do it. Only, we have to mentally count *1, 2, 3, 4, 5* as we talk because each set of five papers should be turned a different way to prevent lopsided stacks.

Deena asks, "Did you all watch that girl on TV last night? The little red-headed singer on *Wee American Go-Getters*?"

Deena likes all the performance competition shows, especially the ones featuring kids. She once told us that the talented kids give her hope for the future, the way they chase their dreams. Tony's fourth chair broke right when she said this. We heard the metal snap and his body slam down onto the carpet. We ran to the front room to help him. We had a whole chair-fail routine at this point. It took all three of us to get him up, two pulling and one pushing. Once he was back on his feet, Deena ran to the back storage room to restock his chair. I gathered chair shards and threw them in the dumpster. Trish checked for injuries. That time, the talented kids/fourth chair time, when Tony was reinstalled in his seat, he looked at Deena and said, "Your love of twirling children and your simplistic hope for the future have given me a fuller understanding of human desperation. Thank you."

Trish and I shake our heads (*stuff stuff 2, stuff stuff 3*); no, we hadn't seen the singer on TV.

"Well, she was a red-headed little thing, about five. She came out dressed in a full-length black gown and wearing lipstick, and at first I was thinking, *Now wait a minute, let these kids be kids. She shouldn't look like a come-hither woman when she's only hip-high.* But then she started singing, and she was a tiny Marlena Dietrich. She was just exactly Marlena. She sang 'Falling in Love Again,' and I got full goosebumps. She did the accent and the throaty voice, and it was like she was mad but enjoying herself. Perfect. She only needed blonde hair and a cigarette. The judges liked her but said she needs to slink around the stage more if she wants to make it to the finals."

Trish and I nod (*stuff stuff 3, stuff stuff 4*), and Trish starts to tell us about the crime procedural she'd watched. A woman wasn't believed, then it was too late.

Tony rises from the chair (with great effort, pushing down on his table for leverage) and walks toward the darkroom. His Sendings are always inconveniently timed. Now one of us will have to switch over to labeling, our overall progress slowed down.

He knows we are thinking about how inconvenient his timing is.

He says, "Per terms, I must give Sendings at predetermined intervals," as he pulls the darkroom's light-blocking cloth curtain closed.

Before Tony, we all had a go-to darkroom joke. Mine was: "We can rent it out as a mini-meditation retreat. People pay big for sensory deprivation." Deena's was: "We can use it to threaten our kids into behaving. *Quit hitting your sister or it's thirty minutes in the dark!*" Trish never quite understood the game. She'd say, "We could use it as a pantry, couldn't we?"

Not a joke, this is what actually happened to our darkroom: A quicksand-walking coworker sent by WHO KNOWS goes in there several times a day to transmit (*SOMEHOW?*) personal and private information about everyone in our town, and the sounds emitted when this happens are like this: *ZEEEK ZEEEK PLUNK, ZEEEK ZEEEK WOP*. We don't know if this sound comes from Tony's mouth or from some equipment he has in there (*WHEN?*) or if the sound comes from the receiver's end. All we know for sure is that it takes only fifteen minutes to report the hopes, grudges, loves, and missteps of two thousand people, which has given *me* a fuller understanding of human desperation.

I move to the label machine and tell the girls about the comedy special I watched last night. "The best joke was about a vegan ATM. It wouldn't accept cash because it refused to eat anything with a face. Get it?"

We all laugh and (*stuff stuff 5*) turn our stacks.

Tony opens the cloth.

"I'm glad to hear laughter. Overall, laughter is down 23 percent this week. This seems to be due to the decline in temperatures and the recent news coverage of nuclear weapons. But we simultaneously believe there's no real cause."

He loves to emerge with a tidbit for us. He must feel lighter after a Sending. I thank Tony for telling us the tidbit. I know he doesn't have to; he offers it to help us. He thinks we're like him, always seeking to better understand instead of avoiding all major truths.

He might never understand humans; we're too simple.

We get our papers assembled, labeled, and into mail bags by 5:45. We'll make it—the post office is only around the corner. Trish and I toss bags onto the back stoop that we use as a loading dock, and Deena, down on the ground, picks them up and gives them a second toss into the van. Tony goes back to the front desk.

I ride with Deena to the P.O. to help her unload. We arrive at 5:49, plenty of time. Deena backs the van in and pops the trunk. Sandy is standing there waiting on us like we're late. She's holding one arm in the other, an impatient pose. I get out, grab some mail bags, and throw them into the empty bins without saying a thing to Sandy. She can pout all she wants, but we've made it in time.

I unload a couple more armfuls, and then I can't help it. "Do you have to stand up there and pout like we missed your birthday party, Sandy? We got here over ten minutes early. Early isn't late, per the definition of 'early'!"

"Per terms!" adds Deena, already laughing at herself.

"Per terms!" I say.

Sandy isn't even listening; she's rolling the full bin inside. This bit is for us. We've never let ourselves joke about all this before.

Deena calls, "Sandy, it's people like you who are killing laughter in this town!"

Sandy is inside at this point.

"Tony told me that Sandy collects racist figurines and dildos made of rare crystals."

Deena smiles. "He did not!"

We get back into the van, slamming our doors one second shy of being simultaneous.

"No, he didn't. He told me she sleeps with balled fists, though. All night they stay tensed up. He says it's not even all that uncommon."

"That's pretty sad."

I nod. "It really is."

But I don't want our banter extinguished by Sandy's agitated sleep habits so I say, "Maybe it's not sad. Maybe every night she dreams that she's a hammer, or a double hammer. Maybe she likes Peter, Paul and Mary, and she's hammering all over this land while she sleeps, and it's very restful and peaceful."

"Yeah, maybe she volunteers for Habitat for Humanity in her sleep. Building houses. If more places allowed volunteers to be actually asleep and dreaming, I think they'd get more participation."

When we get back to the office, Tony is standing in the doorway between the front office and the main room.

"I did not say sleeping with balled fists is common. It is statistically uncommon at 8 percent."

Deena and I are still giggly from the car. She says, "Lay off, Tony. Can't we just enjoy the brief happiness that comes between issues?"

"Historically, no, you cannot, Deena."

We really crack up at this, falling all over each other, despite not knowing for sure if Tony could rip the sky apart as a punishment or as retribution or as a final acknowledgment of human uselessness. It's way too funny. *Historically, no, you cannot, Deena.*

Bulk Trash Is for Lovers

When she felt she had no one, she took a walk and proposed marriage to all the big bulk trash left out on the curb. The biggest discards (desks, coffee tables, couches, night stands) made her feel both sorry and devoted, which was a feelings combo she liked to seek out, as it was as close to a higher self as she could get. Chipped cups, stretchy pants, foodie or nudie mags—the small trash—did nothing for her. Heap it on the mound. But the big bulk trash items were gently hulking zoo animals, once petted, then turned upon. They didn't bite or maul; they were used as intended, no fault, and it ruined them.

She called these walks her "harsh reality parades" but only in her diary, which she planned to burn or eat or slip between sleight-of-hand magic trick books at the library. For today's parade, she wore her stomping boots and silently offered her companionship to a floral sofa that was two days wet from recent torrential rains. Maybe a soggy sidewalk couch would truly understand her need to be completely alone and yet constantly adored. And maybe the shadeless floor lamp right beside it would be someone she could lean on. She touched the arm of the sofa (cold, squishy, officially junk) and wondered if these people had even tried posting to a marketplace before letting the weather and the open air ruin their belongings.

Wasteful. Lazy. Abhorrent.

Yet she had technically done the same with the white recliner that had belonged to her mother's uncle—an ugly inheritance that she kept and used, even though it was not to her taste and even though she didn't think of herself as someone who needed a lever to help her get horizontal.

One evening she fell asleep in the chair while watching too many episodes of a cooking show. It was the one where the ovens have wheels and can run away and hide, so the contestants have to chase their ovens down while carrying their wet batters and doughs. When she woke up hours later, the ovens were still on the run, and she was sitting in a bloody lake of her own making. She got up and stared down. She was upset with the stain, felt it was unreasonable. Her period wasn't due for five days. She shouldn't have to spray and scrub just because her body couldn't keep time.

She changed clothes, and then without so much as dabbing at the splot, she pushed and kicked the chair onto the porch, threw it down the front steps, then lugged it lug by lug out to the curb. Out! She knew it would be courteous, even in the dark, to lay a dish towel over the blood, or to turn the cushion over completely. She was feeling bold, though, and wayward, and she wanted to let the blood shine and offend. Maybe, she thought, someone would think she'd been stabbed and send over a box of chocolate and an encouraging note about healing.

But in the morning she found that the stain had been gnawed away and torn to fluff. Some animal had smelled blood and gone wild. Probably danced and howled and made teeth sounds. This, for some reason, was too much. This was uncouth and actually wrong—her blood was not for that kind of taking. She put a black trash bag over the seat of the chair and taped a note to it that said "SOILED," so no one would try to load it into their pickup and incorporate it into their living room decor.

She felt like explaining all this about the bloody recliner to the floral sofa that was maybe a little bit her fiancée. I have a past, she might have told it. One you might not like.

Then a man in a red coat came out of the nearest house and locked his door behind him. As he walked to his car, she asked him about the sofa and the floor lamp, if they were his. She tried not to sound overtly accusatory but also like she deserved a full explanation. He looked thoughtful, then used his car keys to point at her and the sofa and the lamp. "They were mine a couple days ago," he said, "but now they are communal."

She didn't like the way he used the word "communal" as a synonym for "trashed." She felt this word choice was very bad news for herself and everyone she'd ever tried to love. Still, she waved in a neighborly way when the man with the crushing vocab got into his car.

She couldn't get the sofa home on her own, plus it was ruined and the florals were sickly and she didn't want to sit on it now, in health, much less during some future sickness. She waited until the man drove away, and then, to keep some small portion of her vow, she put her mouth to the cushion and sucked out a mouthful of rainwater. She swallowed it, started walking off, then came back for one more swallow in case this garbage rainwater, out of everything she'd tried or meant to try, was the thing that finally made her feel permanent.

Safe Distances

Gia is in my closet going through my outfits, purses, and shoes and calling them all scores or tragedies. This feels like a surprise inspection, like she's going to put on white gloves to check for dust and sad, bad choices. Gia dresses like she's from a decade I lived through but didn't thrive in. I find the style she and her peers have adopted to be very "ugly on purpose"—brown-heavy, saggy-baggy, much too downtrodden for upstarts—but I don't say that to her because I want to appear open and receptive, even though the older I get the more I feel my heart and my mind trying to slam shut, BAM, dust flying.

I was planning to take Gia to the botanical gardens today (peak bloom for flowering cherries), but the rain kept us home. My husband left early and won't be home until dark, and I've totally cleared my schedule for the week, given myself a short break from barely looking for graphic design jobs while watching that Swedish TV show about blended families.

It's just us. Here. All day. Together. This feels impossible.

So . . .

Let's say: I haven't seen my niece Gia in person for three years, since she was ten, since she came up to my chin, since she was pliant, since she wore bright colors and smiled without first considering whether she should smile and how big and teeth or no teeth.

Let's say: Gia and I spent a lot of time together when she was small. I got down on the floor with her—stacked the blocks, laid the tracks, made the stuffed duck say, "Excuse me, beep beep, pardon me," while it paddled through the pond of pillows. Before I moved five hundred miles away, Gia and I were very close. We were known to each other. She called me Antenna, like Aunt Tina but more receptive.

Let's say: we video chat often, though, quick check-ins to confirm that we still care enough to push the buttons that show us each other's faces.

Let's say: my sister sent Gia to stay with me for a week. Grace was very clear that if Gia stayed at home for the entire summer break, she would do something awful to her daughter, like cut off her hair and slap her with it, or tell her the truth about all the brain problems she stands to inherit. Grace thinks I have endless patience for shitty attitudes because I kept a goldfish named Kickstand alive for eleven years, even though the sight of his little on-ramp mouth made me gag every time.

(Let's deny: any patience I have or pretend to have is only me grinding down my mind the way people grind down their back teeth. If I appear patient, it's only because performing patience has exhausted me.)

Once our plans were canceled, Gia apparently felt the need to find an indoor project *quick* to avoid any kind of knee-to-knee heart-to-heart. She landed on closet raiding, but I have a feeling that she'd have organized my pantry if that's what it took to keep me from probing around in her murky teen feelings.

"What the fuck, is this like a military jacket?" Gia is looking at my jacket like it just peed on her.

"No! It's just that shade of green."

She puts the jacket over her shirt, which is the color of that cheap chocolate pudding disgusting children tend to eat disgustingly.

"These lapels look militant."

"Is that good or bad?" I study her face for definitive feelings about militant lapels; all I see is blinding youth and beauty but also my mother's chin, which undercuts both.

She shrugs, keeps the jacket on. "These lapels are definitely giving me fighter jet."

I lean against the wall of my closet and tell her that actually I *did* start a lot of fights in that jacket, which isn't true but sounds like a cool thing to say in a small windowless room. I've never spent more than thirty hurried seconds in here at a time—crying with the light off doesn't count. In the sustained light, this place feels like a bracketed parade of all the people I've ever tried to be. Awful. I should tear this room right off the house and replace it with an infrared sauna that will get my heart rate into that good zone.

"When did you ever run?" Gia's holding a pair of tennis shoes by their laces like they are marionettes in a marathon.

"I ran! I still run. Occasionally."

"They're all dusty. Look, a thin layer." She shows me the dust on her finger, like I'm not the very one who avoided rigorous activity long enough for dust to accumulate. Next she's wearing a pair of elderly corduroys, holding up the waistband with her hands because her hips aren't done cooking, saying, "If I had a chunky belt . . ."

I can't believe chunky belts are back, but I refuse to go, "Ah yes, I remember the last time belts like that were cool," because I'm convinced that taking an I've-seen-it-all tone will make all my pubes go gray, BAM.

I point to the shoe box with a red snake on it. She sits on her knees and opens the box. The belts are loose, shoved in. "You know, some grown-ups hang their belts from hooks."

"Maybe you should write those grown-ups a fan letter, Gia."

She's not a bit chastised; she's too busy laughing at a thin black belt I once wore over a wrap dress—in hindsight a very "morning television" look, but at the time I felt that wearing *one* accessory made me a fashion icon. She finds a suitable belt (thick, white) that holds the corduroys up, but all the extra fabric has a raisin-like effect on her lower body.

"Hot shit," I say, which makes her laugh. Oh, but now she's studying me. She might take back her laugh, go another direction.

"Why are you being cool right now?" she asks. I know that is an accusation and not a compliment, the implication being that I'm performing coolness as a party trick since it's clearly not my natural state.

"I'm not being cool."

"You are. You're being sort of moony and funny. You're leaning, too. You never lean."

I didn't think she'd notice my private internal shifting, didn't think she would be tuned into the behavior of such a minor background character. I stand up straight and try to look like I've been holding my own weight the whole time.

"If I am being at all cool right now it's because you look like a California Raisin in those pants, and I learned everything I know about being cool from the California Raisins."

"Okay, that's more like it. Corny references to boring shit I don't understand."

* * *

Gia doesn't eat enough protein at lunch, just like at breakfast this morning and dinner last night, but her immune functioning and energy levels are none of my business.

She tortures her cherry tomatoes, stabs for squirts. I ask if she wants something else, maybe eggs. "Maybe," she says, but I won't leave the table for a non-committal response. I, for one, am eating my protein. Bone loss is a concern of mine. In my dreams, X-rays reveal that entire sections of bone have turned into powder, like pixie sticks dumped out in straight lines between my wrist and my elbow.

I swallow my cold lentils. "Too bad about botans."

"Huh?"

"Botanical gardens. Would have been nice."

"Oh. Maybe."

Even as her aunt, I feel like I'm auditioning for the role of "someone she might slightly approve of." And the audition is going poorly—I'll be lucky to get a spot in the chorus or off-stage pulling curtains. I should stop trying to get her approval, I know that, but there's a frantic scramble inside me that's stronger than this obvious red light.

"Do you remember when we all went to the botanical gardens

Christmas deal, and you refused to leave the tunnel of lights? We were supposed to walk through, keep going, but you didn't want the colors to end."

"I remember spilling hot chocolate on my lap and Dad yelling, 'Jesus Christ.'"

"You must have been four. It was the era of your green coat. Your Gumby years. Do you remember that coat?"

"Nuh uh. I don't even know what Gumby is."

"Neither do I, actually."

Gia's green coat had to be put down. She wore it until her entire wrists were exposed and the paisley lining was threadbare. It was thrown away while she was sleeping because she refused to be reasonable. Now she owns a coat that fits properly but that she has, at best, weak affection toward. I count this as a loss. Another one.

"Remember the tall purple boots you wore to your kindergarten concert? You asked for them to be laced backward, so the bow was at the front, remember? You said you sang better with bow toes."

Gia shakes her head (*no boots, no you, no this*). She's right—aunts have no right to get sappy. Wow, look at me, I can't even win the games I play by myself.

She stands and takes her plate into the kitchen. "Why do you have to ask me about when I was little?"

Because that's when you liked me. "If you want a different topic, you could be the one to bring it up."

She washes her own dish—poorly, I'll have to redo it—and asks me if I've ever cut anyone. She's looking out the window above the sink with an unfocused look, not one that would suggest a yearning for violence.

"What? Like with a knife?"

"Could be a knife, could be anything sharp. Could be on purpose, could be an accident."

"Thanks for the leeway."

"So, no?" She's drying her plate with the wrong towel. That one's for hands.

"No, I've never cut anyone. Have you?"

"Not yet." Her smile is a wink. Her smile is a blinker before a left turn. She rejoins me at the table and sticks her fingernail into the crack between the table leafs, sliding the nail up and down the line. "Have you ever punched anyone?" she asks. "Or slapped, I guess. Punched or slapped?"

"I don't think so."

"A slap would be a core memory for sure. What about kicks? Have you kicked anyone?"

I shift my legs beneath the table, uncrossing, crossing the other way. "Not intentionally."

"Not even in the shins?" How hopeful she looks. I shake my head.

"Hmm," from Gia. Disappointment. I've let her down by having hands that stay at my sides and away from my perceived enemies. Maybe this line of questioning is Gia's attempt to get me to admit how awful everything truly is. Maybe Gia is really asking, *Don't you get tired of this long-ass game of nicey-nice? Don't your worst insides ever seep out? Shouldn't they seep out now and then, given all the disappointment and the disconnection and the monotony that erode the glowing hope we were born with? Do you even know how to let that kind of spillage happen? Are you paying enough attention? Any attention? Are you anything? Are you anything at all?*

I'm *not* anything at all, but I remember a time my hands showed up. I put down my fork and try not to sound overeager about sharing my single bad thing.

"When I was in daycare, I pushed a little girl off the top of the slide. Not *down* the slide. The shorter route, over the side. She landed in the wood chips without making any sound on the way down. She may have been too surprised to scream—I was her docile friend. I was a blank nobody playmate. When the two of us played pet rattlesnakes with the jump ropes, she made me take the rope that was missing a handle. So I had two choices: I could pretend that my pet snake was missing a head or pretend it had lost its rattle. I usually picked the missing rattle, which was less fatal but so much more tragic."

"What a little bitch."

"I know, right? I was stone cold. But the push wasn't premeditated. It was like my whole body was dreaming, but my arms were awake and vengeful. When the dream ended, I looked down, and the girl's arm was going counterclockwise."

"No, I meant the other girl was a bitch."

"Oh, Cassie wasn't so bad. She's probably a CEO now. Or a pro golfer. Anyway, Cassie became Castie for several weeks."

Gia smiles, possibly proud of me for being unrepentant enough to make jokes. "So you pushed her because she gave the crappy snake?"

"I only pushed her because I pictured it happening, and then my arms made it happen."

Gia nods, so she either understands what I exactly mean or she is politely demonstrating her active listening skills. "Were you sorry?"

"I apologized. They made me. And I *did* hate the sight of Cassie's mismatched arms, but that probably had more to do with my love of symmetry than regret. I was more fascinated than anything. It had been so easy to cause an event that made people come running. I couldn't get over that. How easy."

"Wow, that's very bad seed. Did you mutilate any animals as a young child?"

Gia's looking at me, really looking, like I'm actually here, like I'm something, *anything* at all. And she's here too, eyes up, engaged. Here we are, improvising, searching for, working toward, and then finding it, landing on it: our new game, our brand new version of "duck goes beep."

* * *

"I ran over my boyfriend's foot on purpose." Gia reaches for a pillow to put in her lap as she listens to me. We've moved to the couch, which feels appropriate—tables are for interrogations, and couches are for confessions. I'm holding court a bit, with one elbow propped on the armrest and the other on the top of the couch, heart exposed, legs uncrossed, a rare open stance. "We were at the lake, on the boat ramp. It was August, so my tan was all set, and I was probably wearing something strappy to show it off. I was driving his truck, trying to lower a hitched-up motor boat into the water. But I couldn't get the boat to stay straight and reach the lake. Couldn't do it. I'd try to lower the boat down gradually, but instead it would veer to the side, and I'd have to straighten out and try again. Over and over, same thing. I don't know why Jared didn't just do it himself instead of getting out and directing me. I honestly think it's because he was in the mood to yell. He kept saying, 'No, Tina. Whip her! Whip her around!' even though he knew very well that I was not the kind of person to whip things around *or* the kind of person who could tolerate being yelled at on a cement ramp while wearing a strappy dress. So, I finally stopped trying with the boat and started angry-crying in the truck cab. All I had wanted to do that day was to sing quietly under the sound of the speed boat motor. I didn't think there would be a pre-test. When Jared came to the driver's side to take over—which maybe he could have done *before* I started crying—I backed over his foot. Well, not the whole thing. The toes. Not even all the toes! Three, max. But it was pretty easy to pretend the whole thing was an accident since I'd spent the prior twenty minutes demonstrating my incompetence. Anyway, he was fine. I put our beer in the grass, put his foot in the cooler. We didn't even break up for another . . . six months?"

"What else?" Gia is doubled over her pillow, doubly egging me on, wanting to hear me get worse and worse. Since I started talking, I've declined quite a bit already.

I've already told her about getting a colleague fired for lying about her overtime, but really I squealed because that lady always commented on how much I ate at lunch. *Is that all for you? Do you not eat breakfast? Are you going to run a marathon later today? Really, Tina, in terms of metabolism, you'd be better off eating half of this now and then having a sensible snack at between 2 and 3 p.m.* Gia agreed she had to go.

I've already told her about going to an estate sale and stealing a wine stopper, even though there was a laminated sign affixed to the entryway coat rack that said the proceeds of the sale would go to Bernice's heart transplant fund. The stopper was a wood-carved lady with a bulbous hat that tied below her chin. Her face was lopsided and brow-heavy, with an expression that said, *I tried to try but then I stopped*, but I liked her full lips and the way her hat looked like a pile of apples, but most of all I liked that she was the kind of woman who chose a bold hat even though her face was already a lot to take in. I bent down to clang around with a box of spoons, pretending to compare this spoon to that spoon, while slipping her into my purse. I don't know why. She was marked at seven dollars, and I had cash, plus cards, plus the single check I keep folded up in my wallet in case I fall into a time warp that leads me to a strip mall in 1996. I felt, I guess, that stealing the wooden hat lady would restore any dignity she'd lost by first being discarded and then set near the salt and pepper shakers and the box of disparate spoons. My phone vibrated in my purse, and the lady chattered against the screen. She was laughing in there, I decided, cracking up at Bernice's expense.

Gia asked to see the wine stopper, and I mined for it in the depths of my kitchen, and she laughed her ass off at the sight of it. Her exact words were, "She's so unfortunate," but even so, she held the lady in her hand for a long time, somewhat reverently, before setting her in front of us on the coffee table, doubling the audience for my confessions.

Even though these stories about my petty, vindictive behavior are piling up, I don't feel anything like shame right now. I feel warm, awake, and proven right. Shame is boring, and Gia's interest is intoxicating. Her listening, wanting these stories, drawing them out means I've had to reach into the throats of my past selves for her, and what I found down there was a feeling of continuity. I've always been sour, sure, but the real takeaway is that I've always been. It's me every time.

I tell Gia and Lady Applehat that I can't think of anything else to tell them. "That's as bad as I've been." Plus my throat is sore. I'm really not used to speaking more than two sentences at a time—usually a one-word response, then an open-ended question as a punt.

Gia looks expectant, even though I've told her I'm kaput. If she were a therapist, I would call this a meaningful silence because the *go on* is implied.

When she was small and I wanted to take a break from our playtime, she wouldn't cry or beg for me to stay. Instead, she would follow me, still holding her plaything (her doll, her hedgehog, her floppy puppy) and conveying the sadness of the toy by holding it at an angle that made its head fall and its arms droop. How many times had I made sandwiches while stuffed animals pouted near my elbows?

I am suddenly convinced, looking at Gia looking at me, that if I don't keep playing with her right now—that if I elbow her away this time— she will never look at me with this kind of open need ever again. If I can't keep going, keep her tuned in, she'll become another hazy, distant adult I know, another person barely pretending to be happy for my benefit, another person nodding along, going right sure sure *absolutely*.

I consider making up an impressively naughty story, a real door destroyer. Something involving a motorcycle and a bad boy? Vandalism? Public nudity? Identity theft? Big game hunting? Would Gia believe me if I told her I'd once taken down a cheetah in its prime?

"I'm thinking," I tell her, stalling. She takes the elastic off her wrist and pulls her hair up and back—one of my favorite human gestures, the choreographed swoop of it—all while keeping her eyes on me. Maybe the stakes of this moment feel high for her too, like if she takes her eyes off me I'll go back to talking about her childhood, like I'll get all emo about the way she used to say "caterpillar" and start treating her like a relic instead of like a person who's rapidly becoming more potent.

She pulls slim tendrils of hair out of her ponytail so that they hang down in front of her ears. I don't know where she learned this kind of *just so*, but I find it off-putting, possibly due to jealousy. Hair sorted, Gia resituates herself, ditching the pillow and pulling her knees to her chest, cannonball-style. "What about a story from when you were my age?"

If I'm going to make something up, this really narrows my options. She'd never believe that I streaked through a wedding procession or pumped a big cat full of lead while I was still in middle school. Surely there's something real down my thirteen-year-old throat I can grab hold of and yank forward for Gia.

Casting back to thirteen, thirteen, one-three. I'm getting acne. I'm getting boredom. Unnamed despair is coming in strong. Friends, yes, intense friendships, your-spit-is-my-spit friendships, but also so much time alone, so much time in my room. Festering in there. Waiting in there. Hanging upside down off my bed. Lighting candles. Doing sit-ups. Reading books. Touching sentences. Warping. Warping inwardly. Melting. Melding. Wanting. Reaching without moving. Questing without going. Getting greedy. Getting gross. Chasing appetite. Chasing updates. Faking decorum. Blocking senses. Becoming carpet. Staying low.

"Oh," is all I say when I have it—a story that feels wickedly bent to me now, so much worse than running over toes.

"It's . . . I kind of don't want to tell you." I have a strong instinct to cover my face with my hands, but I stay locked in with Gia. She's resting her head on her knees, so the tendrils she made are tassels on her shins. "Now you *have* to tell me," she says.

"It was a different time, first of all. And I was really bored. I felt desperate, but I didn't know what I was desperate *for*, so I had to try a lot of things to see if they made that desperate feeling get any smaller."

I still do this. I'm doing this right now.

Her eyes get bigger. "'It was a different time' is always an excuse for something icky."

"It's not all *that* . . . well, maybe it is." I've never told this story before. Not to a partner or a confidant, not to a pet or a stranger. I feel sick, like this rising secret is bad dairy. If I'm going to say it, I need to do it quickly.

"First of all, you need to understand that early cell phone lines were analog, not digital. Cordless phones too. And phone scanners that could pick up these un-encrypted calls were easy to find. They sold them at Radio Shack. Possibly Best Buy. I got one from my neighbor, who was actually also my friend's uncle. That's a whole other . . . he was a . . . he was the kind of guy who'd give a scanner to a child, okay? So I could hear people's calls if they had the right—well, the *wrong*—kind of phone. Most of the calls were super quick, super boring. Lots of food-related calls. *Can you grab OJ? Could you get some romaine? You think two large pizzas would be enough, or should I add a medium for seven ninety-nine?* Also lots of calls about logistics. *How about Thursday at twelve forty-five? No can do. What's your Monday looking like?* Or *Donnie barfed during circle time. Can you pick him up? Bring a clean shirt.* We didn't have texting, so we had to waste our voices on these things. But if I was patient, if I put in the hours, I'd eventually land on a juicy call. Like I heard this guy from my school talking to this hot girl from the next town over—he had to go to the next town because all the girls in our town already knew he was a total ass. Listening to him degrade himself in an effort to charm her, using this fake sweet voice, saying boy band lyric kind of shit like, *Wish I was there so I could hold that hand of yours, girl.* It was glorious, being embarrassed for him in secret. I'm pretty sure my heart glowed. What else? I heard a divorced couple arguing about child support. He thought he should be able to deduct twenty dollars from his monthly payment because he bought their kid some rain boots, and she thought he should fuck right off. Once I heard a marriage end, but that was a surprisingly calm conversation—they were totally on the same page, very kind, totally reasonable—so either they had already done the screaming, had already worn each other all the way down, or they were making a huge mistake. But none of this is the . . . or, no, the *whole fact* of the listening in is totally a bad story. The invasion of privacy. The toxic nosiness. It's definitely bad. But it's not the main . . ."

A pause. I'm not known for my stamina. I rub my cheeks like my head is a genie lamp. *Come out, come out.*

Gia says, "You really don't have to tell me if you don't want to," which I do appreciate, even though I don't think she means it and will possibly cut/kick/punch me if I don't spit it out.

"Of course I heard something I wasn't supposed to know. Of course I did. I heard my best friend telling my other best friend a secret. Deeply, deeply private stuff. Alert the authorities kind of stuff."

Gia lifts her head. "Oh wow. You really don't have to go into this. Seriously, I don't even want to know anymore."

"Why couldn't I have overheard my friend talking to her mom about yogurt or, say, calling to tell her grandma which word knocked her out of the spelling bee? But no, nope. I had to land on the kind of stomach-churning info that put me in a position that I wasn't mature enough to . . . but wasn't I *looking* for the ugliest, darkest talk? Wasn't the whole appeal of the scanner that I could have access to people's emotions without having to be responsible for them? Keeping myself at a distance while feeding on their intimacy, intimacy I didn't earn because intimacy comes from being close?"

"Mom, I said I don't want to know. You're kind of freaking me out."

Exhale. Oh right, that. *Mom.* That's me. That's here and now. Now that the game is over and the spell is broken, I notice that Gia stopped leaning forward at some point, that she's crossed her arms, and I hear, too late, her asking me to stop. I would never be this close to telling my *daughter* such a story, this close to burdening her with my many manic regrets.

"I'm sorry," I say. "I'm done." There's no way to explain to her that sometimes I pretend—rather elaborately, rather wholeheartedly—that she's someone else, someone further from me, so that I can give our old embedded dynamic the slip and become someone who loves her in an easier way, a less worried way, a way that doesn't bug the shit out of her, a way that can lean.

There's no good way to tell her that sometimes I pretend her father is my friend's husband, a guy I'm keeping it innocently flirty with for now but whom I'm seriously considering for an affair, or that her Aunt Grace is not my sister but a foreign-exchange student who once lived with me for six months and who taught me everything I know about lipstick and layering.

I'd rather not admit to my child that, for me, distance is the key to closeness.

I shake my head to indicate that the contents of my mind aren't something I can at all make sense of, much less articulate. Gia sighs and says, "It's okay," as she stretches out her legs and puts them in my lap.

"Remember when I used to get growing pains, and you'd rub my legs?"

"Of course I remember." I'd sit on the floor, bent over the bed, and work on her sore legs until she fell asleep. I think all that stretching and reaching made my right arm permanently longer than my left, but I didn't mind. It was one of the few times I knew exactly how to help her.

I rub her shins now, gently squeezing, looking for knots along the bone. She lets me do this, lets me be this close, so I ask, "Do you remember when we had such awful fights before school? Like when you were five, six? I was trying so hard not to be late again, but you wouldn't get out of bed, then you couldn't decide if you wanted a hot breakfast or a cold one, and you'd stand there with one leg in your pants for five whole minutes, in no hurry at all. You were the slowest. And I was impatient and grumpy, no fun at all. So we'd be screaming, frustrated, hating each other through the whole process, but when it was time to brush your hair we'd put our fight aside and play our salon game. I'd become the stylist, and you'd become me. Two adults. Two friends. Chatting. Keeping it light. While working on your tangles I'd complain about the weather and ask about your job and your daughter, and you'd take this weary tone and say, *Well my job is very busy with emails, and my daughter Gia is so bad at getting ready in the morning.* And I'd say, *Poor little Gia, I'm sure she's trying her best,* and you'd go, *She's not, but I love her anyway,* and then I'd laugh because it was so easy, then, to see how totally lovable you were, and you'd laugh because I was seeing you instead of rushing you, and the rest of the morning would be fine, a breeze."

And my child, my lovable, merciful child says, "Yes. I remember."

Laugh
Riots

Growing and Trying

Enviable Levels

"If you encounter a woman on the street (a stranger but one who looks warm and knowable), and she doesn't smile or look you in the eye, how do you feel? And how would you like that feeling altered? Be specific."

My husband looks up from his book. This is our new nightly routine—we get into bed, he tries to read while I try to make progress on my forms, and two minutes into our separate silences, I interrupt to ask for his input.

He bends the corner of the page he's no longer reading. "How much longer is this form? How many questions total?"

I flip to the back of the form booklet. "546. Total."

"God. And most are two-part questions, like this one?"

"Correct. *One: What's your current level of expectation? Two: Where do you want it to be?* Is the number 546 higher than you expected? Where would that number be for you, ideally?"

"Are we making jokes about the forms now? Because I've been holding back."

"I can joke, but you can't. I need the levity since I'm the one undergoing the procedure."

"But I'm undergoing the forms."

"You're a form *consultant*. Your consultant fee can be . . . secret jokes under your breath."

He lifts up the comforter and whispers into it, then fakes a laugh under there with our knees. Do I expect my husband to make jokes at nighttime? Do I expect him to solve my riddles with me or for me? And should I? I can't tell. I'm tired. I hate all levels of expectation. The forms!

"Very funny. What do you think of this one—walking by an unknown lady and getting no acknowledgment? I don't think that would bother me. Do you think that would bother me?"

"Why would that bother you? But you can't be adjusted based on my perception of your expectations. You have to be adjusted based on *your* true expectations."

"I know. But I want help landing on my own answer. I have to talk it out, bring it to life."

"Do you want me to be the lady walking by?" He's used to this. Acting out the scenarios really helps. He has recently played: a horse my sibling got for Christmas, a boss who thinks I know Microsoft Excel because I told him I knew Microsoft Excel, a cashier letting me know that my card has been declined, and a stylist telling me I have a knobby chin and therefore discouraging a bob, which I'd already told everyone I was getting.

"Yes, thank you." We both roll out of the warm bed. The day's no longer over.

I say, "What's our scene here? Where are we?"

"City street. Afternoon. Overcast."

"Okay, I'll walk this way from the closet toward the chair, and you pass me from the other direction."

"Should I wear something feminine? I could hold a purse." In past enactments, I've dressed him or given him props. As the stylist, he used a comb to point to my chin.

"No, I can imagine all that. But walk like this." I show him how this lady walks in my mind. She sways, but it's not performative. She has loose hips but also somewhere to be.

"Like this?" His version is a mockery of all people who have ever walked proudly.

"No, Dan. That's not it at all. Why don't I be the woman, and you can be me?"

"But then how would we find your expectation in the scenario?"

"We wouldn't, Dan. I was joking." I must tell the doctor to take me down to a level where my husband's inability to register my jokes doesn't make me feel like a shadow puppet hoisted on stage without being lit up from behind.

"Sorry. Show me again." I try a simpler version of the walk. Maybe the way she goes down her hallway. Dan tries it. It's not right, but it's fine. He's pleased with himself. Adds an arm movement. Dan's levels are enviable. His mother only bathed him once a week, fed him a rotation of three meals.

"Places!" he calls. "City street!" At the closet door, I look past Dan and envision skyscrapers and a café. No, a deli. No, a high-end crêperie. An urban farm?

"Jeena?" Oh, Dan's already at the door with me. I missed it. I forgot to see her and feel potentially snubbed or potentially nothing.

"Sorry, can we try again? I had a scene issue."

"You were creating an entire cityscape, weren't you?" He's familiar with my scene issues. When he was a horse, I put him in a heated stable with a rocking chair for guests. But then my sister wouldn't let me inside.

"I might go for a cobblestone street this time, so make her walk like she's trying not to get stuck in a crack. That's a joke, FYI."

"Tell your doctor about this. You shouldn't need so many details in order to imagine a scene. This will be a useful example for her, for your leveling."

"How did you envision the city street?"

"Gray."

"Like a hazy fog?"

"No, a solid gray."

"Like concrete?"

"Like cardboard that's been painted gray. Hastily, with a big brush."

"And that was enough to get you into the scene?"

"Sure."

"Fascinating."

"Thank you."

"Enviable levels."

"Thank you. Let's go again. Try the gray."

From our opposite sides, we go again. I try to see gray, but my gray is foggy and floats away, but then I see a woman a little older than I am. Her style is one I cannot achieve. I can tell from her outfit, expression, walk, aura that she has a lot to say about men in hats, exotic rug placement, sequencing of hors d'oeuvres, and how she too once read the word "footsore" twice in a single day. I want her to see the promise of me too. Then she's gone. Past. Dan reaches the door and turns back around. "Verdict?"

"I'm devastated."

"That a woman you do not know did not acknowledge you?"

"Apparently, yes."

"That's all it takes to devastate you?"

"You can't judge my reactions when we are trying to get to the heart of my levels."

"Sorry, I just can't imagine having that reaction. The people I walk past are gray and don't engage my expectations at all."

"She didn't know me, but in that moment I knew her. She sleeps in fancy silk robes that hit below the knee. She memorizes entire book passages, not to recite but to possess the words. She can sit in a chair and keep both feet on the floor. I want to be that kind of lady."

"I know you do, my love, but not for much longer."

I head back toward the bed. "I need to get some sleep. I'll have to get up early because I forgot to pack the kids' lunches. There's a lot I need to get done tomorrow. The day's not going to day itself."

Dan looks sad about me. "Do you really see days as hulking objects that need to be pulled along by a string?" Instead of expecting an answer, he gets into bed and lifts up the comforter on my side. "Get in. Stop pulling."

* * *

At work, I watch video testimonials on mute with captions. The captions are mostly inaccurate, but I get the gist. "I feel life a new berry baby. I export nothing. I enjoy evening around me."

If you search "LoExa testimonials," you get forty-seven thousand hits. The Lowered Expectations procedure has only been performed 320 times according to their official site (getdownstaydown.org), so almost all of the testimonials are fake. Making fake LoExa videos was a trend for a couple weeks. A pop star made one, even—she sang off-key wearing loafers. They're jokes, but I still find the videos helpful and hopeful.

There's a subset of videos about LoExa reversals, or attempted reversals. Officially, the procedure is permanent. Expectations can be manipulated downward but never raised. Raising levels would be too dangerous, according to the FAQs, even if the capability existed. But people in the reversal videos claim to have undone the lowering. Each extols some homespun reversal method. One woman put apple cider vinegar in her neti pot twice daily for a week and says burning her face plumbing got her back up two levels, so she can at least find a parking space instead of driving around the lot for hours.

It's most likely that she's lying, has never had the procedure at all, just wants to be seen, had vinegar in her cupboard, got an idea suddenly, laughed at her own parking lot joke, probably needs the procedure, actually.

StopTryingSteve posts videos daily. His are my favorite. He's upbeat, and his head moves around a lot when he speaks, like it has been untied from the expectations of a neck. His are not reversal stories. He *loves* LoExa. He's in love with wanting nothing. He says he wakes up in the morning, and his first thought is something like "This is fine" or "I am in my bed" or "Today is happening." It's never "Someone is expecting me to do this thing today, and I must rise and do it" or "My feet are cold" or "Might it start raining around ten and ruin my plans and where is my umbrella—the trunk?"

Steve is a proponent of going down to an extra-low level and hiring a live-in aide. At extra-low level you need someone to brush your teeth, change your sheets, and offer to show you sunrises and sunsets, which continually take you by surprise. This is controversial. Who can afford to go so low as to be non-functional and then hire out functionality? The super-rich, the mega-monied. Steve must be a billionaire, so I should hate him and suspect him of corporate greed, but instead I check back constantly for new videos. He's reassuring. He's consistent.

Some days there are videos of Steve being shaved by his aide. She has to ask him over and over to stop smiling so she can make even strokes. Then Steve is unfailingly astonished by his smooth face, can't stop rubbing his own cheeks.

I want to be astonished by daily occurrences. I want to be mesmerized by the showerhead's stream. But I don't want to *want* mesmerization. I write this notion down on a piece of paper at my desk, then shove it in my purse, which is full of these kinds of notes in hopes they prove useful for my leveling or for upcoming form questions. The other day I went digging through my purse for a tissue and came out with a scrap of paper that said *like a sloth but with more drive, like the soul of a sloth but the duty of a windmill.*

Dan has watched Steve's videos over my shoulder at home, where I can watch with the sound up. Dan finds it easy to hate Steve. He says if Steve's levels are really that low, how can he maintain an online presence featuring daily videos? I tell him the aide must help, must keep him interested in the camera, must record and post.

I only defend Steve because I have a right to spend my attention on stupid endeavors—like watching a twelve-minute video of Steve poring over a wall calendar, effusively pronouncing each month and holiday. After he said "Rosh Hashanah," he got full-body goosebumps. There was an extended close-up of his pokey bicep. But I know that his videos are most likely fake. Hell, they might be paid advertisements for LoExa—Steve a hired performer, the aide a former Shakespearean actor. LoExa *would* want to encourage people to go extra-low level. It costs more.

Someone walks behind me, past my cubicle. I toggle from a video of Steve laughing at his wiggling toes to a spreadsheet. Toggle back to

Steve. His aide has served him applesauce. He exclaims, according to the captions, "Apple you can oat with a spook!"

Another reason to suspect Steve's a fake: men very rarely get LoExa. This fact is not listed on their official site. I read this statistic in an exposé on LoExa. A respectable news source found and interviewed verified LoExa recipients and also scored a source working inside the company. They found that men and women were equally likely to be interested in LoExa, to be receptive to the advertising, and to visit the official LoExa site for more information. It's at the next step that the group divides. When the person goes to their friends and family to tell them they are considering a surgery to lower their expectations, the reaction of the support group determines whether the person goes forward with the procedure. And it seems that a man's friends and family will pull him back from the edge, encourage him not to give up, bolster his confidence in trying again, in trying more. And the people surrounding a woman will say, "Yes, do it, you deserve relief, a break. Let go, you've tried hard enough."

How would I react if Dan told me he was considering LoExa? I hope I'd be supportive of his choices. I hope I'd acknowledge the feelings that led to his LoExa curiosity. But I worry that I'd feel a sense of personal failure—that I hadn't kept him buoyed up, that I'd chosen a partner who is weak, languishing, and unable to live up to his own meager dreams, and why do I have to be the kind of person who loves him?

I take a Post-it from my desk drawer and quickly write: *level where I feel that everyone is deserving of my love, no judgey love that must be earned.* I fold it to go into my purse, then unfold it to add: *but also some people are mean/bad, so I want my level above having to love them.* Then I add several question marks and slip it into a side pocket with my other folded ideas and a reward card from a shoe store I've been to once.

That's lunch. I close the video, turn off my monitor. Lunchtime is for forms.

* * *

Here's what Little Jeena expected for Adult Jeena: creative outlets, a pristine complexion, en suite bathrooms, frocks for frolicking, many many romantic partners to be carefully narrowed down to one or two, friends with good ideas, meaning and purpose, job titles, devoted pets, children who were silent except when expressing gratitude, a linen closet full of high-end sheets, vacation plans, knowledge about houseplants and flavorful sauces.

How did I do? No, nah I'm bumpy, hardly, okay some frocks, not even close, their ideas are so meager, nope, plural? no, no, haha, a stack of cotton sheets underneath my winter coats, never, I barely even tried.

* * *

I brought soup for lunch today. Only now, at lunchtime, do I see the risk to my forms—broth dribbles. In the office kitchenette, I warm my soup in a mug then drain all the liquid into the sink. Dry soup—chicken, carrots, spiral noodles, unblemished forms. At my desk, I get out the forms. They won't fit in my purse, so I've been carrying them around in a cloth tote bag that reads "Fingers Are for Glovers," which I swear I somehow acquired without choosing, without money. I've marked my place. Question 189. I take a bite and chew while I read.

Question 189: How many pillows do you believe is necessary for a made bed? What number is excessive? What amount is paltry to your current sensibilities? And what number of pillows do you suppose is a healthy expectation that will lead to fulfillment around pillows without giving sacrifice to comfort? Do not provide a range; give an exact number of pillows.

I need one, right off, for my head. I wouldn't want to go to a pillow-less level where I'd have neck crooks and headaches. Expectations can't solve the well-known angle discrepancy between shoulder and ear. And then one pillow for Dan. Two pillows, minimum. Oh cute, it's a partnership question wrapped up in a pillow question. Wait, is it? Am I supposed to live alone in this scenario, so I can more clearly define my expectations?

I reread the question. It says "a made bed" and not "*your* made bed," so maybe I'm to consider the number of pillows for a standard generic bed. Like a hotel bed? But a hotel bed might be a special-occasion bed—honeymoon bed, New Year's Eve bed—and certainly special occasions deserve plentiful pillows. But a hotel bed could be a flew-in-for-a-funeral bed or a loveless-affair bed, in which case a scene of comfort might be an upsetting reminder that *others* deserve plentiful pillows, even when you personally are in more of a sad bed moment.

I think I'll write "two" for how many pillows are necessary. For how many are obscene, can I write, "Seven for a funeral bed, and no number of pillows could ever be obscene on a honeymoon bed"? No, can't. The forms, as far as I can tell, have no sense of humor.

I sift through my purse scraps and find my phone. I had hoped to knock out these questions on my own, but I need back-up. I put my phone down, find a scrap of paper, and write *a level where I have the confidence to answer questions without reassurance and guidance from others, but not a level so low that I do not anticipate that others can help me in any way.*

I call my sister. She's a good one to call because she's home with her kids, and although she's busy, she always answers. She usually sounds like she's taken shelter in a phone booth during a hurricane, but she answers.

"Jeena?! Jeena, what's going on? I can barely hear you."

"I can't speak very loudly. I'm in the office. I have a form question. I need your help on this one."

"Is it another one about whether to look at your own reflection when you walk by a window? Because that was really a waste of two hours. My kids had pulled down the curtains and were eating Styrofoam peanuts by the time we landed on an answer."

"Yes."

"It *is* another question about reflections?"

"No, our answer to the reflection question. It was yes."

"I think I've come around on that, actually."

113

"I don't have time to go back and reconsider form questions, Tori."

"How's Dan? Is his knee still giving him trouble?"

"I don't have time to talk about Dan's knee! Listen to the question!"

I read her 189 very carefully, so I'm providing her the exact wording. She says, "Hmmm."

"I'll tell you my initial thoughts," I say, "but I want to hear yours before they become tainted by mine."

"You need four pillows. Two for each person. Five is excessive, two is paltry, but one is worse."

"Okay. What about the healthy expectation part?"

"I think four is healthy enough. Then again, my expectations don't need adjustment."

"Right . . ."

"Two pillows might be fine as long as they aren't those thin, floppy kind."

"Wait, is that why you said four, minimum? Because you assume thin pillows?"

"I guess I do. See! My expectations are naturally pretty low. It's because Mom always told you that you were smart and cute, and she told me I was 'just fine the way God made me.'"

"Why didn't they give us pillow dimensions to work with? We need to know the thickness and the stuffing material." I am getting loud and over-excited. I look around the office to see if anyone has noticed, but no one is at all interested in me because they've never known me to do anything interesting.

"And there're also decorative pillows to consider. TOBY! STOP! GIVE IT TO ME. I SAID GIVE IT. WHERE DID YOU GET THAT? YOU KNOW NOT TO TOUCH THAT! NEVER AGAIN, OKAY? IT WILL BITE YOU! NOW GO PLAY, I'M ON THE PHONE WITH AUNT JEENA. I'm sorry. Toby went into the bathroom and managed to swipe the blade out of my razor and was carrying it around like a prize. I'm not surprised. I should have put it up higher."

"Really? I *am* surprised. How could he get it out? Why couldn't he see it was dangerous and sharp? It seems like he'd know better."

"Mom really did a number on you. 'You're so clever and picturesque, Jeena! Your children will never make poor choices!'"

"What were you saying about decorative pillows?"

"You're picturing plain white pillows, but then there're the ones that go on top with a sham to match the bedspread, and then the small colorful ones for flair."

"Oh, right. And those long tube-shaped ones?"

"Sleeve pillows."

"Is that a term?"

"That's what I call them."

I remember my soup remains. I force a bite of lukewarm, rapidly cooling death. "I'm more confused than ever. I don't know what to answer."

"Go ahead and factor in the decorative pillows," Tori says. "What do you require in terms of decorative pillows?"

"I don't require them, but maybe I should."

"They can't adjust you up, remember?"

"Yes, good. So I'll say two as my current level, and I'll stay with two as my expected level because I don't want a pillowless level or Danless level."

"Done!"

"Thanks, Tori. Mom was right—you're just fine the way God made you."

"Funny. Good luck with the next one. The answer is probably 'it depends.'"

"Bye." I write my pillow conclusions while forcing bites. Cold noodles are less off-putting than cold chicken. I unspiral them with my tongue.

Question 190: Imagine yourself in a classroom setting. The teacher has asked a question. You think you know the answer, so you raise your hand. Three other hands go up. They belong to the smartest people in the class. How do you feel? What do you do next? And what's the preferred response for an ideal you?

A classroom. I wish Dan were here to be the teacher or a raised hand. I close my eyes and try to imagine the whole thing on my own. I'm in a huge lecture hall with stadium seating. I can barely see the teacher. No. I need it smaller, younger. I open my eyes to reset. Take two. I'm in an elementary classroom, in the middle of a row of desks. The teacher asks us the capital of Montana. I know this. My grandma lived in Montana. She had jury duty in Helena once. I raise my hand. Other hands go up. I look around and behind. The hands belong to three adults over fifty wearing navy blue business attire. And headsets— they all have headsets. But I still know the capital of Montana, so I keep my hand raised.

The teacher calls on me. "Yes, Jeena?"

The navy headsets all look my way. I can't say anything. *You think you know the answer.* They seem to be communicating through their headsets, using low whispers. The one in the front row gestures to the teacher, a gesture I don't recognize, one involving both pinkies. The teacher nods, says, "You don't know, do you Jeena?"

I open my eyes. It's 12:30. That's lunch.

* * *

You have a son. His hair color is irrelevant, but it's also brown. He is ten. He is sweet, still sits on your lap. He is also lacking in curiosity—never had a "why" phase. For his school science fair, he completes an experiment testing the efficacy of dish soap. He tests only two kinds of soap and uses one on a metal pan and the other on a glass casserole dish. He is awarded a third-place ribbon. How do you feel about his achievement? About his school? Is this a high point or a low point, him holding a green ribbon and posing beside his poster board? An additional detail: he titled his project "Thanks Dish Soap!" Now, how would you like this scenario to strike you post-procedure? Explain which aspects you want to feel glad about. Designate a place in your home for displaying the ribbon.

You live within walking distance of the library and are in need of an engrossing novel to carry you through the longest days of winter. The sun is scarce. You've been wearing a scarf indoors. You decide a walk to the library is the remedy you need. You bundle up and brave the cold, and it's not that bad, really. You might be feeling invigorated. Inside the library, you go to the "New Release" section and pick up a book because you like the cover—colorful geometric shapes against a blue sky. The blurbs are promising. "A debut that screams whoodie doodie." "A romp of some worth." You check it out and note the due date, and you feel satisfied by its promising weight on the walk home. You make a cup of tea and sit down with your book. The first three pages are a description of light shining into a room. Discuss. You know the deal: now reaction, new reaction.

You have a large glorious tree in your backyard. It provides shade and a habitat for you to engage with. Your own nests! But also, so many leaves. Ten bags worth. It's the beginning of fall, and you must rake the first round of fallen leaves so that the next round is even doable. You scrape your rake around your lawn and form a small pile. After ten minutes of work, you've piled around 5 percent of the leaves. Then a wind blows and leaves fall anew and you're back to 0 percent, as if you'd never started. As you let the setback settle over you, you see that your neighbor's small daughter is watching you from her upstairs window. Do you keep raking? If so, what percent of the leaves do you collect? Do you leave the piles for another day or bag them then and there? Do you keep the girl's attention by dancing a little, dipping the rake, and kissing the handle? INCLUDE ACTUAL AND PREFERRED RESPONSES.

Your romantic partner of twenty years gets you a pricey gift—a gesture they have never tried before. Your partner is so thrilled, cannot wait until OCCASION for you to open your present, instead foists it on you three days prior, while you're still drinking coffee. It's a helicopter tour of the city you've lived in since birth.

You go out to dinner with a group of close friends. You disclose none of your despair. The bisque is too thick. You don't want to have to ask where the bathroom is. React.

You're having sex with a person you've desired for a long time. Your genitals are perfectly groomed. Your back goes out.

You meet your best friend's newest romantic partner. He's anyone.
You buy coffee at the only gas station for miles.
You look up at the sky. What was that?
You buy a rolling suitcase for $25.
You bake a pie for the first time.
You go to a friend's art exhibit.
A cat walks into a room. Go.
You meet your birth mother.
Someone honks.
Polling place.
Swimwear.
Airplane.
OK?
Y?
N?

* * *

Dr. Klausner says anyone who completes the forms definitely needs the procedure.

I've done it. It took three months of form work. So many phone calls, reenactments, forced daydreams. The process of questioning my every expectation in hopes of pinpointing my level has not exactly *lowered* my expectations, but it has them scared and isolated. We've found them, and they are looking flimsy.

Now we meet in Dr. Klausner's office for "next steps." I've brought Dan along for moral support but also to carry the forms. My right shoulder is now lower than my left from the burden of the forms. The ripple effect has had a nipple effect—my breasts are no longer a set or a pair; they're now more like an opening act and a headliner.

I take the forms from Dan's bag and place them on the doctor's desk. She thumps them twice and says, "Great." She doesn't look at them or read any of my answers. Maybe she can suss out my level by hearing the pitch of her thump, like a ripe melon. She puts her hand on them again, possibly to feel any remaining reverberation.

"I'll get to these soon. First, let me tell you what happens next. You've passed a major hurdle. The forms do a lot of people in. Literally. What I need from you now, if you're still serious, are your spouse's signature and permission from a licensed therapist."

"I have to get permission from my husband? And my therapist?"

"As a precaution, yes. It's a legal thing."

"What if I weren't married?"

"We'd need a signature from a parent or sibling. A coworker of over five years is also acceptable. But everyone receiving LoExa so far has been married."

Dan giggles and grabs my hand.

"He'll sign," I tell her. "And I'm already seeing a therapist, so that shouldn't be an issue."

The doctor says, "Okay, signatures pending. Now is a good time for me to answer any questions you may have. Let me quell any fears."

Dan speaks up. "Why should she get LoExa instead of taking an antidepressant?"

He's never raised this question to *me*. "Well for one, I'm not depressed, Dan! I'm expectant! It's totally different. One is down and one is up."

"Let me field this, Jeena. I've answered this many times. People are more comfortable with pills, I get it—they're so small. But drugs—I mean depending on which drug you take—can make you feel numb to what you see. You have less reaction, and maybe that feels nice, maybe that feels better than a bad reaction. But LoExa is not to numb; it's to clarify, to see the world without any pesky ideas of what the world should look like."

I know this is an incorrect oversimplification of medications like antidepressants, but I want to be on her side of this back-and-forth, so I keep quiet and make attentive faces.

"So it's more like a factory reset?" Dan asks.

Dr. Klausner nods. "A bit, sure. Her reactions will not be dampened—her reactions will be refreshed. They'll be unrehearsed. Does that make sense?"

Dan and I nod because she answered the question and not because we understand. I squeeze Dan's hand, and he says, "Go ahead." He knows what I want to ask.

"Doctor, what about going too low? What are the risks?"

"You've seen the videos then?"

"Yes."

"You know they are mostly fakes."

"Yes."

"Almost entirely fakes, I can tell you."

"Can you tell me if StopTryingSteve has had LoExa?"

"I cannot. I *can* say we've had very few cases of going 'too low.' We had one woman with an adjustment a bit lower than we intended because she sneezed mid-procedure. But she's thriving! She's amazed at her two-year-old's hide-and-seek abilities. She finds network sitcoms so hilarious that she was able to cancel her streaming subscriptions. That's a monthly savings! She found a man who neither beats nor hugs her. She gave us a five star rating."

"But wouldn't she give everything five stars?" I ask.

"Exactly. Like I said, she's thriving!"

Dan wants to know about the actual procedure, the specific technique.

"It's a highly calibrated procedure," the doctor tells us. "It's not a crude poke, like a lobotomy."

"Is it a brain surgery, though? Will I have to shave my head?"

"It's not a brain operation, though most recipients expect that it will be. It's a five-point procedure: we go into your gut, fingertips, corneas, and heart. Afterward, we recalibrate the brain by showing a slideshow."

"A slideshow of what?" Dan asks. I'm concerned about the mention of heart surgery, he wants to know what's going on with the slideshow.

"It's a proprietary blend of images."

"I'm sorry, did you say you'll be messing with my heart?" The office feels stuffy and menacing to me now, like the room contains the answers to all my problems, but the answers are brand-new problems.

"Only very little. We partially clog one artery. It's not open-heart. We go in through your arm. I promise it's not as risky as it sounds."

"Yeah, Jeena, the heart stuff is perfectly safe. The dicey part is with your eyeballs."

I frown at Dan. "Sorry. He's worried about me, and this is how it comes out. His little jokes."

Dan dips his head in apology. "I'm 100 percent supportive of Jeena. I'll sign anything. But I don't want her returned with bloody eyes or unrecognizable limbs."

"I understand your concerns, Dan. She'll still be Jeena. We aren't taking anything from her but a cloudy lens. Really, we are only polishing the lens, removing the grime. That reminds me. You'll need to fill this out."

Dr. Klausner swivels around to a file cabinet behind her and bends over in her chair to dig through papers. She places her chosen sheet on the desk. "This is your Extraction Selection Form."

"My what?"

"The grime I mentioned in my lens example—that's the unreasonable expectations, right? So when we go in and clean that off, we must do something with the removed grime, the extracted expectations."

Dan says, "You mean there's a tangible substance removed?"

"Tangible to us, yes. Here's what you get to do, Jeena: you get to choose who will benefit from your extracted expectations. It's up to you."

I pick up the form and read my options. Single dads, corporations, middle school art teachers, people who frequent bowling alleys, newborn babies. I don't need to go any further. "I pick newborn babies. Unless . . . Would that mean they'd end up needing the surgery later?"

"No, no. They're getting the boost so early that they actually have time to live up to their expectations. And we're extremely careful with the levels. Think high school graduate, not NASA. You are doing this at exactly the right time because we've recently figured out how to give the extraction while babies are still in utero. The newborns were always spitting so much of it back up."

"What do the corporations do with the expectations? Just curious."

"I knew you'd ask, Dan. They use them against their competitors. One corporation will use the extracts to raise consumers' expectations about a competitor's products, so that the consumers are then disappointed and won't buy those products in the future."

"How does that even work?"

I squeeze Dan's hand to say, *Really with the questions?*

The doctor shakes her head. "I can't tell you, I'm sorry. I realize it's an ugly practice, but the corporations pay well, and their money enables us to help more people."

"I pick the babies," I say. "Or the fetuses, I guess. Do I get to see a picture of the baby I sponsored?"

Dr. Klausner and Dan look at me like they wish I'd already had the procedure.

* * *

It is afternoon, which is fine with me. I am at the dining room table, which is, sure, a good place for me to be. Through the window, I see a cloudy day. Gray. Splendid. Actually, that makes me laugh. It's Dan's world out there. Hahahaha. A Dan day. Ha. I laugh so much now. My cheeks get sore, but the soreness is pleasurable in a neutral way.

Dan has taped a list to my arm again. I'm surprised to see it there and also thrilled. I move my arm, and the list holds on tight. I'm so proud of it. I have to laugh. The first item on the list says "Print Goldie's permission slip."

I remember, yes. My daughter is going on a class trip. Her teacher emailed the slip weeks ago. But I never check my email anymore. I *can* check it and I *can* read it, but I simply have no urge surrounding emails. There was a form question about this, actually. They found the right email level for me, I can tell. Five stars!

I open my computer and go to my email. Thanks, computer! There's the permission slip one. And I see that an online retailer is having an outerwear sale. Nice of them to let me know. I'm so happy for all the people who need coats, but my current puffer is beyond satisfactory.

I open the attachment from the teacher. Goldie will like the grenade exhibit at the history museum! That's a nice event for kids! I'm printing the slip, but my computer is also talking to me now. Fine!

"Wake up and shake up with Cupman's coffee!" Ah, I get it, a commercial is playing on another open tab. I find the right tab and see a woman drinking her coffee. She's sitting at her table, same as me. What joy, synchronicity. What a nice woman. What a nice mug. The likable mug-woman offers her line to me, smiling. "Because the day's not going to day itself!"

Well. A familiar phrase! My own, even. Familiar phrases, so . . . reassuring. I feel a strong sensation that my body can only understand as an itch. My thigh itches furiously, urgently. I scratch through my pants. Then it's my calf, like a pack of ants. I pull at my hem and see my skin is red and angry. I can't think of why. I can't think of any small bugs I've encountered.

So (itchy!) it looks like my expectations grime was not given to a fetus after all. I am not a fairy godmother, and that's okay. Preferable even. I mean, I've always loved coffee. If my expectations had to be handed over to a corporation, I'm jazzed that it's one related to coffee. Coffee is for everyone. Babies are for two people, four tops.

My very own extraction, showing up right here on my table! How lucky I am to have encountered it! I wouldn't expect my checked boxes to be taken as gospel. I wouldn't expect preferences to survive in the wild. No. I would not.

And the itch quiets down. And the red feels gone.

I play the commercial again. Not to hear my old words but to hear the song playing in the background. It's several voices together, scatting a hum that sounds just like a promising morning.

Full Stop

In 2017, emboldened by the general sense of demise in the air, a fresh crop of abortion bans began popping up across the country. In my state, the governor was holding a special legislative session specifically aimed at further restricting abortion access—his own bonus season of paternalism toward the uteruses inside Missouri's borders. He was having one of those *let's keep this party going* nights, and the good times would be kept rolling by taxpayer dollars.

I received frantic emails from all the pro-choice orgs. The planners had been planning. Busloads of people were going to Jeff City from all over the state—the majority from St. Louis and Kansas City, but a few brave stragglers were from smaller towns up north or southwest or from down in the bootheel, aka "the Show-Me State's Gonzo nose." The plan was to get to the capitol, listen to an array of speakers, and then march right into the governor's office with our message of *How dare you? But also, we aren't all that surprised.* I decided to join them.

After putting my information into an online form, I received a text with the name of the person who would be driving me two hours west to Jefferson City. I had hoped to be given a seat on the bus leaving from St. Louis, where I could put on headphones and listen to podcasts while the college students and retired women had a lot to say to each other. Most other women in their thirties were working (paid or unpaid) and needed to stay put. I had kids to take care of (unpaid) but also had a supportive husband with a flexible schedule—so with advance notice I could get out of staying put.

This wheely volunteer was named Winona Rasterson, which sounded like a nickname a saloon fella would give his gun. I thought, *Oh fuck, what if she's one of those people who take pride in being "real straight-shooters"?* I knew I couldn't take two hours of her calling it like she saw it. I imagined showing up to the governor's office holding a sign that said, "I was forced to listen to someone rant for ninety minutes about the way their groceries are bagged, a rant I *had* to endure in order to get here to the capitol and demand that you trust women to make their own decisions, and now here I stand—infuriated in every goddamn direction."

I found her Facebook profile. Winona was perhaps in her midfifties. Based on her photo, I guessed she would be talkative but also generous, like she'd have a box of Kleenex in the floorboard between us and would gesture to it if I sneezed. She had good teeth and hair that saw a stylist often, which indicated a certain income and also some reassurance that I'd be in a car with up-to-date safety features.

She was tagged in a black-and-white photo of a home with a wraparound porch, and she commented, "I remember." She posted an update after her brother's surgery, the gist being that it was over and they were feeling optimistic and thanks to the cousin who brought sub sandwiches. Nothing political. Actually, she did post a photo of a candle, which *could* be a reference to any one of the hateful, deliberate tragedies that half the country insists are merely a string of confounding coincidences.

Her profile contained a website link. The site was her-name-dot-com, and the page was impressive, professional. No pop-up ads for Petco. Her photo looked like the work of a legit photographer, someone who knew how to play up the hair and the teeth for all they were worth. I learned that Winona was a longstanding, successful voice actress. She'd recorded over seventy audiobooks in her home studio, which (according to the photo gallery) she'd decorated with seashells and arrowheads in alternating rows: a point, a curve, a point, a curve.

The "listen here" tab offered audio samples of her vocal styles: a medical narration, a cozy mystery book, a corporate instruction video, a sci-fi novel. My kids were at school, but my husband was downstairs, and for some reason I bristled at the thought of him hearing the voice actress samples. I went into the bathroom, turned on the exhaust fan, and sat on the stool my children used to reach the faucet. I picked the "contemporary" recording first because I wore statement jewelry and a lot of bold collars. Winona's contemporary voice was like that of a news anchor when talking about her pets or her weekend plans—controlled and to the point but with that deliberate veer toward folksy relatability. *Yes, friends, even I—a person in a blazer—must pick up dog poo with a baggie hand.*

I clicked on every available option. Winona was soothing, then authoritative, then conversational, then concerned about my hair loss. Why did *she* get to have an array of personas and a whole career that fit inside a square soundproof room? I found myself impressed with her and unimpressed with myself—an adult hunkered on a stool under an exhaust fan.

* * *

When Winona's car pulled up to my house five days later, I still hadn't decided whether I was going to let on that I knew who she was. Or who her *voice* was—the voice employed by both Procter and Gamble and Joyce Carol Oates!

I opened the passenger door, and as I got in, she said my name. I wanted to record it to play back when introducing myself to new people, like, *Wait, let me hand this over to a professional.*

"Candice, it's so nice to meet you." She pronounced "Candice" like it was an exclusive restaurant she'd used her clout to get into.

I said, "You too, Winona" and was too aware of how I'd tried to match her voice quality and was I perhaps mocking her? Winona's car smelled like marker fumes mixed with pastry, like fresh-baked Sharpies. "Thank you for the ride. So nice of you."

She nodded, said "no problem," and then dug through her tote bag until she pulled out a road atlas. She had the correct page marked with a scrap of paper that had my name and phone number on it. She'd even put parentheses around my area code.

"So . . . we are going to take I-64 over to I-70. Would you mind holding this and telling me when to turn? I've highlighted our route. And written all the turns and exits in the margins."

I was holding an atlas that belonged to the voice of the grandmotherly elf who gave Americans a rousing speech about eliminating odors at family gatherings in a beloved Glade commercial that ran each year from November to January. I should have asked why she didn't use GPS, but one, she was a celebrity, and as an American, celebrity was the one authority I respected, and two, she was a volunteer, and when someone gives their time they are free to give it in the manner in which they see fit.

When we paused at the stop sign at the end of my block Winona said, "I've disabled the GPS on my phone. The last thing I need is the government keeping tabs on my whereabouts or Merck and Pfizer studying my habits to see if I develop the cancer they're trying to cause and then cure!" She waved for a pedestrian to go ahead. "So what about this nutty governor we've got?"

I thought about opening my door and tucking and rolling out into the street while we were stopped. I was on a car ride with a conspiracy theorist—trapped in her mindtrap. I took a long breath but through my nose, so it wouldn't sound like judgment. *This is not a big deal. She simply has some off-kilter ideas about her phone. And our phones are ruining our lives. Keeping a skeptical eye on the government and big pharma is prudent, to a degree. Remember, this is a woman who has competently and convincingly read passages written by our nation's top biographers. But wait, hasn't she also lent her talents to huge pharmaceutical companies?*

"Do you need me to direct you to the highway?"

"No, I've got this part down. I go to a monthly poetry reading nearby so I know the area."

"Do you write poetry?"

"No. But I like to keep my finger on the pulse."

Help help help.

I was hoping to save the Kid Card until at least Chesterfield, but I panicked; as we gained speed down the highway on-ramp I told her my kids' ages and interests and the last funny thing they each said. ("I feel like the stairs are the only place my legs can really show what they've got." "Get a grip, Q-tip." "Stop always stopping me!")

She said they sounded darling, but I wondered if she was suppressing the urge to say their lines better than I did, better than they could. I wanted to ask her about her own family and living arrangements. I don't tend to ask women if they are married or have children because asking seems to imply that I think they *should*. And if they do have those people in their lives, they often float to the surface naturally. *Oh, my son told me I shouldn't drink through a straw because it causes gas bubbles. Sorry, that was my husband calling. The garage door again!* But I wanted to hear her speak at length, a live clip of her "highway driver" voice.

"So, do you live with anyone? What part of town are you from?" I added the second question to soften the first, giving her the parachute of an answer so specific she could respond by pointing.

I was getting hot in my sweater. I started the negotiations with my seatbelt and buttons as I waited for her answer.

"I have a place in Clayton. I swear it's not as swanky as it sounds, 'a place in Clayton.' I rent an apartment—throwing my money away, gladly. It has these braided archways, but the wood floor creaks something awful. It's like you're causing the building pain."

I finally had one arm free, cooling down. I'd had to push my shoulder blades flat against the seat and reel my arm into my sleeve slowly. The seatbelt alarm was dinging, but we were pretending it wasn't. "So do you try to stand still when you're home?"

"The kitchen is tiled, so I like to be in there."

I waited to see if she'd answer the first question. I couldn't possibly repeat it without seeming like I had a label maker in my purse with the words "Old Maid" already imprinted on plastic. Instead I made a big show of folding my sweater and putting it in the floorboard.

After I fastened my seatbelt she said, "It's just me . . . in the apartment. My daughter moved to the Bay Area for school years ago, and she comes back as little as possible. It had been the two of us . . . but I guess she didn't like that." She paused while a car passed us, as if they might be listening in. "Maybe the whole time I was saying, 'It's us against the world, sweetheart,' she was thinking, 'I'm on the world's side.'"

Her voice didn't sound hurt. She sounded thoughtfully worn down— not toppled with one whack but disassembled piece by piece. I almost wanted to tell her that *I* would be on her side. I felt protective of her voice and of the wraparound porch she remembered, of her face when she pulled up ten minutes ago. But she didn't know I knew most of that. "That sounds really hard."

"I don't blame her. If I'd ever had the chance to leave anyone, I might have taken it. Do you want a snack? I made soft pretzels. I thought knotted dough was sorta symbolic of this special session."

I was not hungry, but I couldn't refuse her meaningfully twisted snacks. This was a bread-based way I could be on her side.

"Can you grab them from the backseat?" she asked. "I try not to be a distracted driver. My goal is to die lying down."

The basket of pretzels had been bedded down with a red-and-white kitchen towel. I handed one to her, and it felt warm, like freshly shaved skin. I chose my own pretzel and covered the rest. There was a baked beans can full of black Sharpies in the floorboard behind her seat. It was wide and heavy enough that (apparently) it didn't spill on turns. That's how many baked beans it had held. That's how many Sharpies Winona required.

I turned around and took a bite. The bite was chewy and salty and reminded me of the mall at Christmastime. Long receipts. "These are great. Thank you."

Winona said "pretty good" with her mouth full. Her pretzel was already three-fourths gone so she must have shoved that thing right down her money-making talker. This delighted me. I thought, *Hey, she's great, who cares what she avoids and what she keeps the pulse of?* And then, *Maybe I should stop evaluating people, situations, life, myself on a moment-to-moment basis.*

"Why do you have so many Sharpies?"

She sat the last pretzel bit on her thigh and wiped her hands on her pants one at a time, keeping a grip on the wheel. "For impromptu protests. I also keep cardboard pieces and poster boards in the trunk. Did you bring a sign for today? Do you need to make one?"

"I wouldn't know what to write." Admitting this felt personal, but so far the drive's revelations had been one-sided.

Winona swallowed her last bite and repeated the phrase "I wouldn't know what to write" in a way that better conveyed how much I cared about the big issues but also how paper-thin I felt, how overwhelmed. Then she added, "'We will not go back' works for most protests."

She turned on the radio. I got us each another pretzel. Once we stopped talking I thought about what we'd already said, the hidden meanings, the cumulative effects. I assumed Winona was thinking about what was coming, what we were driving toward.

* * *

I woke up when we pulled off the highway. I was incredibly thirsty. Too many pretzels. Winona said, "Almost there. I *think* I took the right exit . . ."

"Oh, I'm sorry! I never sleep in the car . . . or during the day . . . or in public."

The music had been turned down to a hush. She'd adjusted the whole car to my sleep—navigating on her own, quieting the music, lowering the A/C. She may have even reached back for her own pretzels, risking an upright death.

"Can you . . . ?" She pointed to the atlas on my lap.

"Of course. Where are . . . ?"

"We're on Highway 54."

"Got it. Sorry. Your next turn is the McCarty Street exit."

She repeated, "McCarty Street exit" and hit the consonants extra hard. I wondered if the real reason she didn't use GPS navigation was that the staccato computer-generated directions offended her sensibilities as voice talent.

* * *

"This is it. We just have to find parking . . ." As Winona looked for a space, I stared at the capitol building, which I hadn't seen since a civic-minded middle school field trip. (They took us to a putt-putt place with ice cream afterward, as an apology for trying to teach us something.) It didn't look like a place where rights were given. The drab dome had a real "taking away" feel—a sucking, a regression, like your ears might pop when you walk in. *We won't go back!*

We parked and I thought, *I want to stay in the car*, like a moody tween at a family reunion. Winona got out, went to the trunk, and came around to my window with a yellow poster board as big as my arm span. I grabbed a marker from the middle of the can, the pistil of the Sharpie bloom. We'd never stood together before. Our heights were similar but only because her shoes had heels and her hair had authority. She handed me the poster board; I was glad because without something to hold onto I might have tried to give a hug I hadn't earned. I took the yellow poster board to the hood and wrote, "LISTEN TO ME! I STARTED AS A HEARTBEAT!"

As Winona and I approached the building, we saw a group posing for a photo on the steps. Four rows, a busload from Kansas City—their signs said "KC hearts PP." They tilted their heads and showed their teeth, and I felt sad about the camaraderie and sense of purpose people find when begging for basic rights and fair treatment. How demeaning, how inspiring.

Winona said, "Hey, you wanna go be in their picture?"

"Seriously?"

She started climbing the steps in a diagonal line toward the group. I hesitated but then followed her. She was my ride.

She went to the very back and hoisted up her sign, which said "NEVER AGAIN" with a drawing of a wire hanger. I felt a little disappointed—the old tired wire hanger. (It's all been done before—in back alleys, broom closets, atop kitchen tables covered in microscopic chicken DNA.)

I reached the photo op a few steps after Winona, but I was too late—the group was disbanding. The second-to-last photo would have a mystery woman in the back, and the last photo would contain a blur to the side—me, deciding too late that I had something to offer.

* * *

Inside, organizers handed out paper programs and told us we were congregating in the rotunda.

I said to Winona, "I feel a little rotunda after eating all those pretzels."

She puffed out her cheeks, filling them with air. This seemed out of character, a reminder that I didn't know her at all. Then she said, "Be careful. If you look pregnant someone here might chain you up and monitor your growth."

We followed people we assumed were heading to the rotunda. It was probably in the center, at the natural bulging place. The rotunda was grand and spectacular and yet (yawn yawn) standard, stark, and devoid of neon. When I saw this as a twelve-year-old, I had a simple/ sleepy/white feeling that the adults in this building had the situation under control and everyone's best interests at heart. I also thought, as a child, that all wars were finished, that America had defeated racism with one march, that a woman would become president any minute and that maybe it would be Murphy Brown. I don't know whether I was a dope or if I had a low-quality education, but I think if someone had said, "*Listen*, Jim Crow laws were in effect when your parents were born," I might have had a better understanding of the country I had been born into.

Rows of folding chairs faced a small dais with a podium reading "OUR Special Session." The dais was flanked by staircases that were absolutely *begging* for descending Rockettes or brides or debutantes or some sort of well-behaving, flat-bellied female who sticks to the script.

I pointed out a cluster of empty seats near the back. I was eager to sit down and be a fixed object in a swirling building of mixed opinions. Winona was craning toward the front of the room, where the organizers were chatting and surveying the turnout. "I think I'm supposed to sit near the front."

I asked, "Why?" but she had already walked away. I resented her assumption that I'd follow her and her car keys anywhere, but then I hurried to catch up. I knew her two hours more than the other attendees.

I joined her in the very front row, even though sitting in front felt too eager and made me extremely leery of crowd participation. (As a kid, I saw a play where the actors came into the audience to make people dance, and I've yet to unclench.)

"You don't have to sit up here with me." Winona's tone made it clear that I was being a baby but that I was a baby with free will. I looked around the room and tried to focus on my reasons for being there. I watched the people milling around, making friends, holding signs under their armpits, clutching water bottles, using the designated hashtags. I thought about the governor and his support of fake clinics that cheated women out of accurate, comprehensive health information. I thought about all the tasks and plans these people had to put aside to be here. I thought about all the senators who'd never spent a dreary January day all alone with a baby. I thought about the senators who *had*—maybe they ran for office to support the welfare of women and children—and what they were up against. I thought about shitty grins. Rousing rage is my one true talent. I can summon my anger the way newborns can fall asleep—anywhere, at once, and deeply.

I reignited myself into being a glad attendee. The president of one of the local Planned Parenthood or NARAL chapters opened the ceremony. She talked about how much money the governor's special session cost per day, how if the governor were truly interested in lowering abortion

rates, he would expand Medicaid and support both accurate sex education and access to contraception. She recapped our reasons for being
there right as we got there, which was a satisfying and galvanizing
welcome. I felt so grateful to her, to others like her, who devoted their
careers and time to this cause while the rest of us dealt with our reproductive organs quietly in office bathrooms and school stalls, hovering
in gas stations while holding purses on bare thighs or in the downstairs
half-bath with a toddler watching.

The woman said, in conclusion, "Please welcome our first speaker—
Winona Rasterson, a voice actress and audiobook narrator from St.
Louis."

Winona got up and left her sign and her purse with me. She turned
around and smiled, and everyone stopped clapping right as I decided
to start. I had been too busy reeling.

"Welcome." The word silenced my incessant inner chatter. I felt
warm, expectant, and focused.

Winona said she was going to tell us about her abortion but that
she had to start further back and work her way toward it. I noted
that Winona was using her "cozy mystery" voice, which was either a
choice or a clue.

She had married young, nineteen, a nice enough guy. They had
dated for a year, and she didn't actively like anyone else, so she said
yes. He had asked her father for her hand, even though "if he'd asked
my dad to answer any additional questions about me, he would not
have been qualified to answer." Once married, she left college, but her
husband finished his schooling. They soon had a daughter. Winona
stayed home with the child. There was no discussion around this. The
marriage, dropping out of school, having a child—she said she chose
all of it by not doing otherwise.

"I didn't know how to locate my own interests and desires, my own
well-being, much less say anything *out loud* about them. My parents
didn't exactly foster a strong sense of self or autonomy. When I was
three, my father pushed me down a tall slide because he had decided I
was too old to be afraid. I cried and screamed, tried to hold on, said no,

I didn't want to do it. He pried my fingers loose, shoved, and I landed in a heap at the bottom, crying even harder. My dad said, 'You did it! You went down the slide all by yourself! You had fun!'"

Winona said her husband was gone, mostly, working for an airline. She was an involved and enthusiastic mother. By age two her daughter could recite many nursery rhymes and even knew the phrase "moist towelette." When her daughter started kindergarten, Winona got a part-time job waitressing in a diner. She pointed out the year was 1987 so that we could adjust our mental image of the diner accordingly. The diner had a rotating pie menu. "You didn't need a calendar. You just had to look and see which pie was on the counter under the glass dome. Lemon meringue, oh it's Tuesday again."

I sensed a cliff we were all about to fall over. Winona was hedging in pie, lingering over the funner details, perhaps holding herself back from telling us the pie for each day of the week.

"I liked working. We didn't need the money, really—I spent my paychecks on fabric for my daughter's clothes and put the rest into a Christmas savings account. I was making friends. The girls I worked with incorporated me into their circles. Being in these circles with people developed enough to *have* and *express* opinions helped me realize that I liked and disliked certain things (likes: cigarettes, cunnilingus, Anne Tyler novels, dislikes: pantyhose, sex standing up, Updike). One friend encouraged me to take classes at a community college. I scaled back my hours at the diner and timed my classes so that I was still home when my daughter got off the bus. I was working toward an associate's degree in communication. My daughter thought it was funny that we were both in school. She'd pretend that I, too, needed permission slips and would sign her name to strips of paper and stick them in my notebook."

Winona smiled, remembering, and I wanted to call her Bay Area daughter and deliver some firm-worded updates.

"This man . . . he was dating one of my friends, a fellow waitress. He was a regular at the diner—owned a flooring business, never ate his top bun. I was telling him the daily specials, and he interrupted to ask if I'd like to do a voiceover for his local flooring commercial. I agreed. I didn't have to pursue, choose, or ask for the opportunity—none of which I was capable of back then. I did the commercial and was told I did well. I guess he sold some laminate. That led to other commercials, plus a couple radio spots. I was *good* at this voice work. I had a skill. Something I possessed on my own. And then . . ."

Winona looked at me. I nodded twice. *You can do this.* It was one of the few occasions where I had the correct impulse at the right time.

"I found out I was pregnant. And it did not feel like happy news. It felt like a screeching halt, a wrecking ball, a regression. I loved the time I'd spent taking care of my daughter, but I didn't want to do it all again. I didn't want to give up my new life right as it was beginning—a burgeoning career, my classes, my community of friends. I looked in the mirror for a long time. I thought she would tell me what to do. But she was not me. She was the part that can be shoved, the body. The part I needed to ask was inside, my voice, the part that I'd recently found—the part that tried to tell my dad what I didn't want before I was shoved and told how I felt about being shoved. This kind of voice-denying action, repeated over and over in various situations, ended up shoving my voice down so far into me that I no longer had to bother with refusals and pleading. I became easy to lead, like a broke horse, toward water I was not thirsty for.

"I asked the woman with the recently uncovered voice if she wanted a baby. She answered 'no' and sounded resolute, sure, brave, but not without sadness. I felt the decision land in me, to choose my own course this time, to not have the baby."

Winona cleared her throat down into the podium but wouldn't look up. I thought, *Even here . . .* , but then she lifted her head.

"I chose to have an abortion. I wanted to share my story today because stories like mine are less gripping to recount and sympathetic to hear. There is no tragic arc. I was not raped. My health was not at risk, nor was the health of the fetus in question. I was not destitute or alone or poor or hungry or scared. I was a comfortable, healthy adult woman with considerable privilege, and I chose to end my pregnancy because I did not want to have a baby. That is *enough* of a reason to have an abortion—my voice told me no. I do not have to list the pros and cons I weighed or tell you whether I was on birth control or if I considered adoption. When I say I don't want to do it, that's what I mean, full stop!"

There was applause, and I participated right on time. Winona glowed with found assertion. I don't think the last part of her speech had been prepared. She got there through spontaneous feeling. The tone she used in the second half of her speech did not correlate with any clip available on her website. She should make a new category: click here for "glowing assertion."

As the clapping subsided, Winona thanked the audience before leaving the dais and returning to her seat beside me. Without looking at me, she put her hand on my kneecap to quell any questions or requests. A settle-down gesture. (My grandma used to do that to me in church, wordlessly conveying that I was fidgeting too much, that I should sit still with my feet on the floor and let God's word penetrate.)

I minded her. I settled down, asked nothing, and looked at the dais, where the next speaker would become indignant in a worse, warbly tone. But before Winona could take her hand away, I grabbed her thumb and squeezed it. Less intimate than holding hands and more encouraging than a double tap on the wrist, I hoped it said, *I saw you do that.*

A couple of the speakers fell into the "tragic arc" category Winona mentioned—women with pregnancies that weren't viable but who had to wait, unnecessarily and painfully, to end them, thanks to restrictive abortion laws. A doctor spoke, a lawyer, a young woman who had never been pregnant and was fired up in that try-and-stop-me way.

Once the speaking portion of the event had ended, we were to eat a box lunch and then storm the governor's office. This felt like a backward sequence as I do my best storming on an empty stomach.

When Winona said, "Let's eat" and walked toward the line for food, I followed. People kept stopping her to comment, to thank her for speaking, to share their own stories. I was jealous of these people who got answers and smiles from Winona instead of the old knee-stifle. I tried to stand close to her answers and responses.

Once we were in line, and her admirers were busy with sandwiches and their phones, she finally explained her omission. "I didn't want you to be nervous for me. You strike me as the nervous type."

I nodded and bobbed and said "fair," but I wanted to know the exact moment she knew this about me. Was it right when I reached for her door handle?

She whispered, "Do you think I should have mentioned that my husband left me over the whole ordeal? It's important to my arc, but it felt good to edit him out."

I knew she didn't *really* want my opinion. She was already looking ahead at the front of the lunch line, trying to see who was getting what she wanted.

* * *

Winona and I ate on the floor of a walkway while leaning against a wall. We sat on our legs so we didn't trip any allies. No one was permitted to eat in the rotunda because of the potential risk to the ceiling paintings, as if people throw their crusts into the air after a meal like graduates with their ceremonial caps.

As we chewed and made friendly-but-darty eye contact, I thought of my own questions and comments for Winona but decided against sharing them.

Did your husband actually say, "Keep the baby or lose me?"

My own reproductive history is three planned pregnancies and three healthy babies, but I had a heck of a time figuring out how to use tampons.

Have you met any celebrities during your corporate commercial gigs? The Keebler elves? How about Snap, Crackle, and Pop or that risk-averse gecko?

What's your daughter's phone number, area code first?

All I said was, "It feels good to be *doing* something instead of shaking my fist around the house."

Winona looked over her shoulder at the organizers, who were eating standing up. "I can't wait to take this show up to the governor's office."

I thought, *Really?* because it rarely occurs to me to look forward to anything. She must have felt my reticence because she added, "Aren't we here to make a fuss? To be heard?"

I nodded, telling myself: *You came here to make a fuss and use your voice and not to allay your own anxiety by doing as little as possible (mostly a bunch of sitting) so later you can tell yourself, "Well, I tried." Right? Right? Right?*

* * *

I lost her during the march upstairs. She rushed to the front, her voice harnessed and ready to lead. I didn't try to keep up. I wanted to watch from the safety of the wayback. I liked my meeker counterparts in the rear. We had gotten ourselves there, and that in itself was a feat for us waybacks!

The governor's office had an antique-looking sign hanging over the door reading "Governor's Office, Welcome," which was an easy lie. The sign looked like it would creak like a weathervane if pushed to swing. The hallway smelled like an art museum.

Outside his door, we held our signs high for no one and chanted, "Not the church, not the state. Women will decide their fate" and other rhymes of blood consequence. Every so often I'd see a flash of Winona's shirt up front. I wanted to zoom in on that flash of Winona to find answers, meaning, and encouragement about my being there and about the potential of my own voice.

The governor did not emerge. I couldn't see into his office, but I assumed he had at least one secretary stationed inside who was trained in finger-wagging and in dismissing the stories of those personally affected.

A front-line protester produced a megaphone, which she must have been lugging around since way back in the rotunda. She yelled with enhanced volume right into his doorway, "COME OUT, COME

OUT, COME OUT." Everyone joined in. I yelled too but privately felt that the chant COME-ON-OUT, COME-ON-OUT would have made a better cadence. I scanned for Winona. There. She was not shouting, only staring at the woman with the megaphone. I watched her reach over and snatch it from the woman's hands. Winona brought the megaphone to her lips and resumed the same chant with a direct, resolute intelligence it had lacked before. The crowd became louder and more meaningfully confident under the new leader.

Winona professionally commanded the governor to come out for at least ten minutes. Finally, one of the organizers pushed the megaphone down from Winona's mouth and hushed us all quiet. She said, "Great work! Now we are going to tape our signs to the walls to make sure he hears our messages! We've got a lot of tape. Raise your hands if you've got tape. Thank you, tape people! Find tape and pass it on. We've also got markers and paper so everyone can leave their mark. Brianna, raise your hand. That's Brianna with the markers."

Everyone lowered their signs and shuffled around for supplies. The hall echoed with the smacky-stretchy sounds of masking tape. The shift from "shouting heartfelt demands in unison" to "arts-and-crafts time" did not seem to feel abruptly demoralizing and infantilizing to anyone else. To me, the futility smarted. Hard. The governor would never read those signs. They'd be torn down in three minutes flat and probably wouldn't even be recycled.

But being the compliant person I am, I tracked down the tape and put up my sign. It was surrounded by signs that said "TRUST WOMEN," which in our present circumstances seemed like an advanced directive. Perhaps we should have started with "SEE WOMEN" and worked upward from there.

People looked proud of their easily removable graffiti. Some made sign after sign after sign, wanting to take up more and more wall. Was this their voice? We came from all over the state, shared stories and opinions with one another—further convincing ourselves but not convincing anyone new, nor anyone in power. We were not granted an audience with the governor. Instead we were taping up signs, like what we'd wanted to do all along was pass notes. There may have been a few short articles in the news about OUR Special Session, but we'd be presented as fringey busybodies. Those wackadoos yodeling about their bodies again! *Don't worry, no one heard it!*

I stood, without a sign or chant, watching the walls fill with bumper sticker pleas. Then Winona was beside me. She did not look proud, sure, or satisfied. She had returned the megaphone. She hadn't taped her sign up. She was holding it down at her side, with the words facing her leg.

I could only deal with my own demoralization, not this. Not hers. I had to leave. I passed all the people, all their art supplies, headed down the stairs, snarled past the rotunda, walked the halls that led toward sunlight, descended outdoor steps, stepped over yellow parking lot lines, moved toward the row of parked buses. It felt good to move, to leave. Maybe *my* voice was in my movement, was in getting the hell out.

There were six buses. I planned to ask each driver if they were going to St. Louis. I only had to ask two of them before I found a bus going home, which felt like a fortunate pardon.

The Right Light

I eat my lunch in the park because a televised doctor told me to. I should experience the outdoors for at least twenty minutes a day, so my eyes can take in a non-screen light source. He said this letting-in-of-the-right-light will help me sleep more soundly, make better choices at the vending machine, and defecate in shapes that seem to please Mother Nature herself, based on the recurrence of such shapes on land and underwater.

The park near my office has a lone picnic table near the playground and a pavilion housing six more picnic tables. I choose the uncovered table, so I get max sun and don't have to worry about looking unlovable, as a single soul under a roof meant for forty tends to look.

I always bring the same food—a bag of tortilla chips, a cheese stick, and a banana that I slice as I eat, so it lasts more than three bites. I chew one chip at a time and peel the cheese into strings. I eat slowly, so it's clear I'm here to eat, which I prove true by spending the entire time eating. If I gobbled, here I'd sit, unlovable with my wrappers and my peel.

As I make my food last, I watch the playground children fall and cry and hide and seek, and I think about the nature of nature. A skinned knee gets you a patted back. A "tag you're it" gets you some respect and personal space, which you give away as soon as possible. A kick in the head from the patent leather shoe of a swinging girl gets you a glossy lesson in who deserves what.

I squint at all of it because sunglasses would only diminish the very light I'm seeking. If I gave in to sunglasses, I'd have to make up for the lost exposure by drinking my coffee on my front porch in that first-light sun. I prefer to spend my mornings cooking dinner, so when I come home from work I have more time to watch television in the dark. When I am tempted to shield my eyes during lunchtime, I think of my precious after-work hours—meal warmed, blinds drawn, bra thrown, feet tucked, laugh track, auto-play, no one. It's perfect, those hours spent with people who cannot see me. Undoubtedly worth the time squint.

Today there are only two playground children: brothers who came to the park to find new, non-sibling playmates—ones whose breakfast bowl levels they didn't have to eye to ensure equal filling, ones who didn't make triumphant faces when they got a hug from their mother. When no one else is at the park, the brothers go underneath the rope bridge and begin slapping the bare arms across from them. Their mother says, "Well, we can do this at home" and loads them back into the car.

I squint at their car leaving and wonder which of the brothers she secretly sides with during their quarrels. Half of the slaps smart her own arms, while half the slaps sting her own palms.

I cut myself a big hunk of banana. Why make it last when there's no one here? Plus, doing a lunch-based one-woman show for no one would make me appear unlovable to the sunshine and the trees. I'm chewing the gummy hunk when I see a woman walking through the grass, past the pavilion, and toward the park's monument. The monument is an old military cannon that must have some local historical significance. The cannon was shot by or shot at someone who once lived around here, and now we must consider this past projectile while we picnic and kite-fly and monkey-bar.

The woman has a duffle bag. I slow down my chewing to accommodate her presence. She sets her duffle down on the monument's plaque, slides off her sandals, and puts them in the bag. The fabric she wears seems smooth and light. It looks like one long piece has been cut into a tank top and shorts, seamless. The woman looks like a chic monk. I squint at her haircut, blunt.

She touches the cannon right where the hurt comes out. I don't know the term—its trunk, perhaps. She keeps her hand over it, blocking any emissions. Or taking the brunt of them. Then she takes her hand away and starts walking. She's circling the canon. I realize I've stopped eating.

The woman has done two laps and is still going around. Now she's walking with her arms up. Is this tai chi? Now she's pumping her raised arms. Is this a protest? She is keeping a steady pace. Is she counting? Is this a meltdown? I'll keep watch.

She goes around so many times I stop feeling surprised. Instead, I feel increasingly upset. This is not how we behave. We walk with purpose, one way, arms down, toward what we want. And if we must pace, we do it at home while talking on the phone about the steps we are taking to get out of the funks we're in.

Her face is neutral, which makes sense because she has nothing to look forward to. She's headed to a spot she has just been—doesn't even have a tail to chase.

The wind blows her silky top and the two flags above the monument. She walks against the wind and then with the wind, over and over, and I feel all wound up. Is she condemning me somehow? Are her movements calling me a sit-stiller and a know-nothing? Can she tell that no one loves me? Is that why she circles the monument instead of circling me?

I look back at my rations. I hold a tortilla chip and make it go around and around what's left of my cheese stick. This is calming. I choose it. I say when.

I look back at the chic monk lady, and I choose her, too, as an experience to have. You. You don't stop. That's something to opt into. I try to instruct her, telepathically, to switch directions and walk counterclockwise. She doesn't vary, but I am with her now in spirit. Watching her is not that different from watching my nightly TV. The chic monk, the sitcom characters—none of them turn to look at me while I watch them keep going.

The more circles I see her complete, the more I need to see her circling continue. I'm pulled in. I'll defend her to anyone. If she were making money somehow, this display of hers wouldn't seem odd. If she were wearing a MATTRESS BLOWOUT sign no one would stare. I eat a fistful of chips. She raises her arms straight up and spreads her fingers, but she doesn't look up to see the sky through the spaces she's made. Her gaze is soft, front-facing. If I could look into her eyes, I feel like I could see the laps she's done and the laps she'll still do and see that they are all one lap.

I am lulled into considering that this woman is engaging time instead of fighting it. She's inhabiting time. Look, she's become part of the breeze. Her movements remind me of the squirrels who run across my roof, zipping for the sake of it—because there's empty space and because they have the legs to fill it.

I wonder why we aren't all pacing.

I look at my phone. I have about twelve minutes of my lunch break left. I bet you really know a minute when you spend it pacing, when you're in lockstep with the seconds. Twelve minutes of trying not to look as unlovable as you feel goes by in a snap. This whole past decade of my life feels like two Mays, one three-day weekend spent in the car, a month inside a bathroom stall, and six back-to-back Christmas dinners.

The TV doctor who talks about the right light also says, "How you do something is how you do everything." I hadn't understood what he meant. I thought he was talking about posture—if you stoop in the office, then you stoop often. But now I get his meaning: This is it, buddy. The present is at hand constantly, and what are you going to do with it? How you wait in line at the post office is the whole shebang. The way you behave at the buffet is a full indictment of your entire being, so scoop your baked ziti accordingly. So how I spend my remaining twelve minutes is how I live my life. I let the word "now" make the rounds inside me. Maybe the word "now" even pumps its arms.

I stand and stuff the rest of my food back into my lunch box. I take one step and then another until I've gone completely around the picnic table. Yes. I keep going. It's such a tight track, I'm always turning. The walking and the turning become a trance. To move without the burden of progress. Going nowhere while being here. My throat feels more open. The ground feels harder. I don't look, but I can sense her movements while I complete my own. We feel like the same speed and the same animal, and I understand moments for the first time—now, now, now, this here. I choose it all, and the moment swirls around me. I am the axis. She is the axis. We keep going. And the light I'm taking in no longer feels prescribed. The light is being received.

Wilderness Mound

The wind is upsetting the trees, but the wind is not upsetting me. The house I built can handle the blows—I made it squat and slightly rounded, so when it's windy, all I really have to worry about are trees being blown onto my well-designed home. I thought about cutting down all the trees in my vicinity, but that seemed preemptive and shade-taking.

Truth be told about the slight rounding of my home: according to its bones, it's a simple four-room wood cabin with the standard corners that form when you attach flat surfaces. I went to the dump in search of anything that would dome my home; I refuse to give my money to those home improvement stores who use chemical pesticides, who spray their own poison when asked to pay for their employees' birth control. I salvaged a truck bed full of carpeting. There was a big heap of it, several rolls, enough to mound my roof. I guessed that the carpet came from a church sanctuary, based on the shade of red. Getting the carpet heap up on top of my house required three disciples. It was hard not to think of the crucifixion when I hammered the red to my roof. I put a tarp over all of it, then staked the tarp to the ground. The visual effect is one I call "restricted mushroom." The practical effect is one I call "impractical." I suppose it's no home-and-garden cover feature, but the wind is not upsetting me. The tarp was to keep it all dry but also to keep the sky from seeing what had been done with the carpet. Of course I don't believe in God, but I do believe in in-kind punishments. The wind comes from somewhere.

For further storm preparedness, I made a shelter out of Concrete Cloth at the foot of my bed. Concrete Cloth comes in a roll and feels like burlap until you douse it with the watering can fifty times. After getting wet, the cloth hardens into an indelible, gray, waterproof, fire-proof eyesore. I use the shelter as a storage trunk, covering its cast-like texture with an afghan my ex-sister-in-law made when she was on bed rest with the twins. (Those two didn't turn out to be worth much. She should have stayed completely upright.) If a spring tornado blows in, all I have to do is chuck my fleece pullovers and quilts out of the concrete chest and then burrow inside with an elbow crawl. I should really do a drill to make sure I still fit. I've gained weight, seemingly all in my chest. My breasts are fuller than they've been in twenty years—when I chop wood they react to the downstroke, a bounce after each thwack. Eighty-two is a ridiculous age for a breast resurgence. I can't imagine who I could possibly feed or entice.

Maybe, if a tornado comes, I'll stand topless on my roof and offer to let it suckle, see if that ends the winds.

I bartered my acupuncture services for that roll of Concrete Cloth. I treated a man in overalls for vertigo, indigestion, and palpitations. His throat was bright red and his cuticles were flaky, so I could tell he ate food out of Styrofoam containers and barked at women, children, and bike riders. Based on his pulses, I'd say his heart meridian had been blocked since he was as young as five. Maybe his mother put him on the school bus without preparing him for his first separation. Or maybe—like all the other fellas I treat out here in the sticks—he'd simply smoked cigarettes, eaten meat off the bone, and avoided saying sorry for fifty-some years, and his heart finally felt pestered enough to protest through arrhythmia.

His name was Chuck, and considering I'd never run into him at the tiny two-aisle health food store in town, he was likely sent here against his will. I imagine that conversation went like this: *Just give her a try. Even if it's hocus-pocus that don't do ya no good, at least you'll have sent an eff-you to that city boy Dr. Hendrix and his expensive prescriptions and his liberal-leaning magazine offerings like* Time *and* Newsweek *and* Women's Health.

I do feel uncomfortable that the rising anti-science, anti-expert, anti-intellectualism out here is a boon to my business, but I figure I'll die before the biggest shit hits the uppermost fan in terms of our crumbling society. Instead I focus on my garden—straight rows of self sufficiency—and on the stacks of cash I keep in tissue boxes.

I've already done my fighting back. I did all kinds of 1960s shit. The only marching I'll do from here on out is to the outhouse and back, bypassing the chiggers. And toward death, if I can find it when I'm ready. I'm not ready to die right yet. I get around fine, I have a hearty appetite, my fingers are still able to work the needles, I can read with my readers, and it turns out my breasts are dancers. Plus the cash and the potatoes keep on coming.

For a long time—decades and change—I lived to battle and to truth-tell. In the morning, it felt like I woke up pressed against a wall of worthy foes. I got out of bed scowling, making claws, and saying, "Yeah, *me*." I was after big pharma, the tobacco goons, those evil fast food slingers, and most of all Monsanto—the corporations knowingly polluting people while tricking them into enjoying the poison. People say things like, *That bowling alley can't tell me not to smoke. Smoking is who I am!* No pal, it's who Philip Morris wants you to be. Being weak and dependent is not a noteworthy personality trait. We're all pluggin' up holes to feel better, so a pack-a-day habit isn't exactly your calling card. It's more like your pick-a-card-any-card.

During those fire-breathing years, I used my needles and my know-how to undo those behemoths' damage one riddled body at a time, while also writing a detailed book about their crooked business dealings and the exact effects these substances have on our systems from a five-element acupuncture perspective. I even had a source inside Monsanto—this guy I met at a Howard Zinn reading who turned out to have a nephew in their corporate office. The nephew was able to get me some flyers they posted in the bathroom stalls. The flyers were announcing a company picnic, but the point is that I was privy to their goings-on.

My book was going to blast, expose, and course-correct, and man oh man was I propelled by the thought of completing that manuscript, which I did. I wrote it by hand until all the points I wanted to make existed outside of me in a form I could hand off. But it didn't sell. No interest, no market, no callbacks, no takers.

No one can think about the big picture anymore, about the connectivity of systems, about being a money-spending, self-poisoning cog in a capitalistic machine. Everyone thinks it's some coincidence that their soda magically appeared at the gas station next to their cigarettes and snack cakes and their fossil fuels, and that the convenience of their downfall is a hoot and a holler, so God bless the modern age—except for vaccines . . . because who knows what they've put in *those* things.

I've let it all go, for the most part—the crusade, the book, the idea that anything can get better. But at night, I allow myself to read small bits of the chapters I wrote. There's one on Nabisco, one on Nestlé. I am not allowed to edit or add to my book, only to underline what's already there. I'm done wasting my energy. My arm is tired of ringing the bell for people who can't even cop to having ears. *Not having ears is who I am.* Fine buddy, go down easy, see if I care. If the doomsday survivors find my book among the ruins and say, "She tried to warn us," it will not be a haughty victory for me because, in truth, I didn't try all that hard.

Giving up the fight felt like a gift to my tongue and to my bowels. I could taste bitter foods again. I could talk about the matter at hand without tying it back to corporate greed. My shits grew by a curve.

* * *

I'm filling up the tea kettle for my midmorning tea. There's no one coming for treatment today, but there's no day-off feeling to be had. I don't keep set hours, or name days when I'm open and closed. People call me on my landline phone, and I tell them "come" or "don't come" or "tomorrow morning, unless you're short of breath."

Today my granddaughter is coming, not for treatment but to visit—although that child needs to swap all that refined sugar in her diet for unsulphured blackstrap molasses. And based on her forehead hue and the scleral show of her eyes, it seems that her earth element is sucking up and dominating her water element. But Tallie won't let me treat her, ever since I did the Kidney 1 point on the bottom of her foot when she was four. Tallie remembers the poke, but what she doesn't remember is the resulting disbursement of energy through her body, which left her invigorated enough to dig a hole in my garden using only a wooden ruler and then bury her treated foot in the hole to show me it was "back to being hers."

Tallie is my only son's daughter. I have four daughters and the one son, spread out over twelve years and three fathers. My son's father is the one who helped me build this cabin, and by helped, I mostly mean he bought the supplies and fucked me in the evenings. The son we had together is named Ray, and he's the only one of my five children who comes around with any frequency or calls on the phone without a clear objective like, *Where's my birth certificate and what do you mean it's buried in the yard and isn't state-issued?* Ray calls to tell me what he's done, or what he might someday do, and how he feels about all of it. He's the only one who needs me, who seems to genuinely enjoy my company, and this is a little too bad because he's the least dynamic and inspiring of my children. The girls want nothing from me—perhaps even avoid me—which makes me long for them, even if only to provoke them into saying mean truths we'd all have to sit with.

Tallie is fifteen, so I don't yet know where she falls on the scales of offspring interest or offspring need. Will she hold my interest? Does she need me to nod along to her class schedule? We will have to see. I *did* admire the way she reclaimed her foot. And when she was twelve, she called me a "grumble cunt" right to my face when I told her she didn't spend enough time reading or moving her body meaningfully. I wrote the phrase down. I wanted to go back and use it to title my chapter about the effects of dough conditioners on uterine function, but instead I jotted the words on an envelope scrap, underlined them, and taped the scrap to my headboard. Every night I think, *Good night you old grumble cunt*, which I consider to be the gentlest prayer I know.

* * *

I turn off the kettle and step outside when I hear Tallie and Ray coming up my gravel driveway, which in addition to being long is also uneven, steep, and prone to washing away. If there's ice or heavy rain, I'm pretty much stranded, but this is a setup I've chosen. Knowing that I could be cut off at any time helps me endure the social interactions I *do* have. *Sure, this lady with the chronic tinnitus who goes on and on about her church dinner menu while I needle her is indeed bothersome, but the forecast calls for a three-day downpour, so I'll soon have a pause from this and all other bothers.*

Ray and his wife have been divorced for a decade. Tallie can't remember her parents touching each other or laughing together about her precociousness. Instead, she remembers needing to perform the precociousness two separate times and trying to muster up the original feeling to keep her performance fresh for the secondary parent.

After the split, her mother, Susie, used her primary custody to relocate them to Little Rock, four hours south of here. Ray only gets to see his daughter every other weekend, and the time they spend together has a forced holiday feel (restaurants and putt-putt)—the kind of stuff that's more fun but ultimately less meaningful than school drop-offs and conversations in pajamas. This loss comes up often during his calls. *Mom, I just want to see her bedhead. Watching her walk up with a careful ponytail is devastating—my own child being presented to me. I miss the little things, like having to search under the couch for her left shoe.*

He moved down south to get closer to Tallie—past the Missouri line but barely into Arkansas. He didn't move all the way to Little Rock because he was hesitant to get too far away from me and my shrinking proximity to death. So now he lives in a town without his daughter *or* his mother, hanging window blinds during the day and calling his daughter and his mother in the evening, telling them about the blinds and how he wishes he could be closer, which he could—to one of us—if he were more decisive.

I wave as the car climbs the final hill. Ray waves back and smiles like I'm the kind of mother who's going to run up and wrap him in my warm apron. What a smile it is, even from here, even with these dying eyes. He really is worthwhile. Thoughtful, sensitive. Just a little too tuggy and unsure for my taste. My boy is wasted on me. Think of all the tender mothers with gruff sons who never ever call—we all need recast and redistributed.

As a child Ray made countless wreaths, collecting the twigs from our surrounding woods and then bending and twisting them into circles while sitting cross-legged atop the picnic table that his younger sister's father had built. It was charming, his rustic craft. Some boys kill snakes with rocks. Young Ray presented each wreath to me with his head bowed, like it was the first one he'd given me, like we didn't live in a cabin with only one door. The stacks of gifted wreaths became so tall that I finally relocated them against the outhouse. I thought the wreath tower really spruced up the ole poo-hut, but once I moved his wreaths he never brought me another. In hindsight, I could have kept *one* and put it on the door. Fine, sure—I'm realizing that my withholding nature could have something to do with his noodly, sad-eyed nature. I'm not so stubborn that I can't connect cause to effect. Cause and effect, heart and lung, metal and water, mother and child. I see it. I'm trained in connection—it's my livelihood, my condition, my worldview.

"Mom!" Ray steps out of the car, and he's so clearly pleased to see me. I feel an unwitting lifetime apology in my hips propel me toward him. I come up fast and put my arms around his neck, like I'm a wreath and he's a cabin door. "Ray," I say to his chest, "you made it."

His body is stiff, probably because I've never run toward him, much less embraced him in such a full-bodied fashion. This flourish of reception surprises me too. Some blockage in me must have been released. There will no doubt be a counterbalanced consequence somewhere in my body. Hot damn, I hope this welcome hug doesn't leave me constipated.

Ray relaxes and pats my back. Then says, "Mom?" like a question and pulls my shoulders back so he can see if my face is the same face that he had grown up with, or if perhaps it was half-slack and this was less a hug than a close-vicinity stroke.

I nod to show that I am fine and also to shake some composure back into my head. I stand up straighter, but I keep my hand on Ray's shoulder.

Tallie, leaning half on the car and half on the open passenger door, says, "Grandma, I've never seen you be affectionate before. It's worrying."

"Good to see you too." I take my hand off Ray and use it to beckon Tallie toward the house. "Come on inside. I made tea."

"Oh great, your famous dirt oat tea." She closes the car door and joins me as we walk toward the house.

"It doesn't taste like dirt! The problem is that your palette has been distorted by artificial flavors and food dyes. Anyway, it cleanses your liver."

Tallie is wearing boots that could harm someone and telling me that she prefers to cleanse her liver with pep talks and daily affirmations.

Instead of coming along Ray has stayed beside his car, observing his untouchable darlings, basking in our inter-generational banter. I lock my arm with Tallie's, for Ray's benefit, to encourage him to be a person who walks toward the action, to show him that I like what he's made.

* * *

Tallie opts for water, but Ray accepts my tea. When I hand him the mug, he thanks me so earnestly that I have the urge to shove him into my Concrete Cloth shell—he cannot be walking around the world that wide-open and vulnerable! He'll end up living alone at the state border, hanging vertical blinds in a roadside hotel. I withhold *you're welcome* as a life lesson.

Tallie asks about all the aunts. She knows where the action is, and it's not the sibling she came from. "Is Aunt Deidra still in Nicaragua?"

"As far as I know. She only calls on my birthday or if there's been a tornado nearby. She signed up for a weather alert for my zip code, so now she calls to make sure I've not been blown up into a tree in my nightgown."

"She's still there," Ray says. "I talk to her every Tuesday. She has a new girlfriend, and she's pregnant."

"Pregnant? Isn't she too old?" Tallie is only fake-shocked, but she's clearly thrilled at the opportunity to open her mouth extra wide.

"She's only thirty-eight!" I tell her. "I had Valley at forty-one, and she was my easiest labor and quickest recovery. I was out tilling the garden the day after she was born. The blood I dripped was a boon to the topsoil. You should have seen the tomatoes that summer! But wait . . . how did she get pregnant by a girlfriend?"

Ray traces his mug handle with this thumb. "Those two updates are unrelated."

I laugh. "It seems like they might end up face-to-face at some point. Has Deidra had girlfriends before?"

Tallie perks up. "It's not a big deal for her to have a girlfriend, Grandma!"

Ray laughs a single note. "You don't need to lecture this one. She had a girlfriend for a couple years in the early seventies. She also once treated the hand cramps of an entire lesbian biker gang, free of charge. So calm down." Ray's defense of my open-minded credentials makes him flush red and look quite handsome, less like his father, less likely to falter.

"That's true," I say. "Kathleen still sends me Christmas cards signed 'your Kath.' I probably would have taken up with more women, but I didn't want to give people the satisfaction of being a full-fledged lesbian after they made such assumptions when I wore a fur vest from ages seven to ten. I guess all those people are dead now. Maybe I'll invite Kathleen over for the solstice. Wait until she sees these new tits!"

"Grandma!" I worry that Tallie is part of a generation that only participates in conversation when shocked or offended. It's very one note: gah! gah! gah!

"She's joking, honey," from Ray.

"I'm partly joking. But know this, Tallie: breasts are a journey, not a destination. They come and go, so try to enjoy all their stages. Right now mine dance while producing naught, but one time I squirted breast milk at a hornet."

Tallie takes a deep breath, perhaps trying not to picture two perfect antennas gummed up with white. "What about the other aunts?"

"Let's see," I say. "Valley works in a factory that makes small parts for fighter planes. Death bolts! My very last baby, supplying the military industrial complex with her bare hands."

"Mom, you know that Valley is a journalist, right? She's working there undercover to write an exposé."

"Are you sure about that? Because I specifically remember her telling me the details of this job. She seemed to enjoy telling me, knowing it would set me off."

"Yes, I'm sure. I talk to Valley all the time. We're incredibly close."

"Close in what way?"

"In the way I'm close to all my sisters. The sharing-our-feelings-and-our-lives way."

"You are?" I hear the realization in my own voice—that my girls are indeed knowable, only not to me. "I *did* know that she was a journalist. I went to her college graduation. We had tacos afterward. I guess I thought she'd . . . you know, changed course."

"I guess she forgot to give you all the details." Ray is speaking in tones appropriate for fallen horses. He probably uses these tones when he talks to his sisters about me; it's his "family glue" tone.

Tallie says, "*I* knew about the exposé."

Ray shoots Tallie a "cool it" look, which makes me happy for him. A "cool it" look is a step toward the daily ease he's been wanting. I have an urge to take Tallie's boot and hide it under the couch for Ray to find when it's time to go.

Tallie apologizes by shifting gears. "Dad told me you wrote a whole book."

"He did?" I say this too quickly and brightly, like someone called roll. The book dream is so dead that hearing someone speak about it feels like a Man Booker Prize. Or a write-up in *Mother Jones*.

"He told me it was the biggest, most ambitious exposé ever, and that's why no one would publish it. He said industries would topple."

Ray looks at me like he wants to dip me in gold and put me on his mantle. The way he sees me as a crusading back-to-land truth-teller makes me feel embarrassed for all the effort I have ever exerted. My crusades didn't make anything better, so there's no reason for him to be proud. All that trying was angsty wheel-spinning, and the mud I kicked up only kept people away. *Everyone stay back, her mission is as long as her driveway and as messy as her affections.*

Oh, all of it so easily becomes pathetic from this view—this son's devotion, this wet mounded roof, my handwritten manuscript, the daughters I don't know, the industries that won't topple, the bowling alley smokers, the vest I took off, the rampant unchecked misinformation, the gah! gah! gahs! stopping nothing, the cities, towns, and country cabins full of blocked hearts, way too many to treat. Nothing can stop the downward slide. There's not enough Concrete Cloth or family glue to hold us up, not in my shed, not in my tender boy, not in Missouri or Arkansas, not in the whole faltering world of fire, water, earth, metal, and wood.

"Oh Ray," I say as I pour him more hot water. I want to ask, *What's going to become of us?* But instead I set down the kettle, plant my feet, and say, "Maybe I should come live with you."

"Really?" Ray can't help but beam at his mother, even though he knows there's a huge part of her that wants him to wipe the beam off his face. Tallie puts her hand on his, a gesture that might mean, *Don't get your hopes up, Dad. She's wiley.*

"Sure. I could find a place near yours, treat a whole new batch of splotchy corn-syrup-addicted Ozarkers. But listen, I want you to promise that when I die, you'll bury me on the Missouri side."

He agrees so easily that I want to ask him for another: promise that after I'm gone you'll keep telling people I was *something else.* But I want to earn this honor from him first.

Thanks for This Riot

Folding used newborn onesies is like stupid-easy origami but with faint poop stains. I tell this to new trainees, and if they wrinkle their noses at "faint poop" I know they aren't going to make it here. Aisle Six is all faint poop, arranged by severity of shade. Further onesie-folding instruction: take one arm and two ribs in toward the chest, take the other arm and two of the other ribs to the chest, condense the crotch, then go in half—a baby sit-up. No swans emerge, only flat stacks that babies outgrow immediately.

Other resale shops might roll up onesies like deli tray ham, but this is the way we fold here. Anita, the owner, is firm on folding. She says, "You can't stack rolls! I refuse to make pyramids on this back counter. What if we elbowed it? Toppling, rolling. Disaster."

We typically buy forty used onesies a day. We used to accept only ten per day because there wasn't a huge market for them. New parents wanted to buy pristine neutral-smelling clothing for their upcoming babies, who they assumed were going to be considerably less leaky and distressed than the babies they'd seen in the mall food court. We'd sell the newborn onesies to moms who were on their third or fourth babies. We could probably sell *them* two mismatched washcloths sewn together, and they'd cut out the leg-holes themselves.

But two months ago, this influencer called The Effortless Peppercorn posted about how she had found a method to never touch or wash soiled baby clothing again. Instead of scraping and soaking the stained garments, she would instead buy huge quantities of used onesies for a quarter apiece, and if her baby had a blowout she'd simply throw the outfit away with the disposable diaper. She hashtagged the post #greenliving, #thriftymama, #wastenotwantnot, #buyused, #effortlessnessstrikesagain, #momsfindsolutions, #every-onehasaquarter, #hacklife, #bodyback, #nowyoutry, #cleanhands, #trashdaycantcomesoonenough.

Now we get her devotees (nicknamed EffPeps) coming in and buying up our whole onesie supply. I want to tell them that they are putting a lot of effort into their effortlessness *and* into our landfills, but instead I smile and double-bag and tell them their baby looks like Fred Astaire, and they say, "Oh, thank you" because they cannot recall his face, only a GIF-length flourish of his legs.

They named this place Infant Replay without me—*way* before I started working here. Like eighteen months before. If I'd been in on the naming, I would have voted for a simple, straightforward name like Preloved Kid Clothes and encircled the whole name with a braided multicolor heart. Puns are for hair salons and the saddest gas stations on the highway.

But I proudly wear the name tag that says both "Infant Replay" and "Leona" because having those words attached to me helps narrow down the options of who I am to be. Parameters I'm paid for. I put on my tag, and I see the day's path ahead of me—I am to be an employee of Anita's, and I am to buy and sell in order to clothe the children of my community, and I am to do this until 4 p.m., and I'll deal with who I become at 4 p.m. not a moment before 4 p.m.

Today Anita is taking her son to audition for a reality show about kids who make pop songs using only plastic salvaged from the ocean. The show is called *Ocean Trash Bangers*. She's left me in charge of the shop for the first time. She said it like it was no big deal. Like, "Thursday and Friday I'm out, so you're in. Drayden has put a lot of work into learning 'Bennie and the Jets' on his Mello Yello accordion, and I can't let him down."

So I'll be opening the shop and training a new employee all on my own. I've trained employees before but always with Anita over my shoulder repeating everything I say in a more authoritative voice. I'll say, "The swimwear goes here." And she'll come over and say, "Swim goes *here*" and point straight down at the spot, then jiggle her wrist so her bracelet doesn't fall off.

I've been dreading this day, which will forcibly widen my parameters. I *like* that Anita tells me what to do. Her prescriptions for my body enable me to be thoughtless. After 4 p.m. I lose all structure, all sense of how-it's-done. This past Wednesday night, I sat on my bathroom tile and had to restrain myself from calling Anita and asking her what people do with their time. *Is it cleaning? Am I supposed to be scrubbing on an hourly basis? Is it list-making? Cooking from scratch? Back scratching? Backpedaling? Front crawl? Can I go ahead and start my morning shift tonight? Take me back and put me in, Anita—before more of the nothing happens!*

In order to sufficiently dread my first day of leadership, I made an event in my calendar for today named "Ocean trash finds another way to fuck us." This joke was less funny when it popped up this morning at 7 a.m., day of the being fucked.

We open at 11:00. I need to arrive at 9:00. My trainee is coming at 9:15. I hope my black Keds look authoritative. I put on the one bracelet I own, so that I can pull off Anita's pointing gestures. I practice pointing here, here, here. My bracelet has a Betty Boop charm. I've had it since I was eight. Why should an eight-year-old wear a curvy, flirty sex symbol on her wrist? Why should a twenty-nine-year-old wear a cartoon character on her wrist? I pull Betty off the bracelet. There was maybe a one-week span the summer I was twelve when I had the exact childlike sultriness to have worn her admissibly. What an unsavory week. I've suppressed it.

I leave home at 8:40 and hope the drive-thru line isn't going to make me late. I need a big drink with a straw for two reasons. One: I've admitted that I'm powerless against my use of plastics and all non-biodegradable materials. Two: The culture of Infant Replay dictates that everyone must have a big drink and place it in the far corner behind the front counter. I call the corner our "thirst trap" but not aloud, which makes it a better joke because it isn't groveling for laughs—it's simply making me slightly less sad.

With my sweaty Diet Pepsi between my knees, I pull into the strip mall where Infant Replay sits between a toasted subs place and a tax prep place. I've never been inside either of the neighboring businesses, but I've thought about applying to one of them so that at 4:00 I could simply go next door and be told what to do until bedtime.

I take a deep breath before getting out of the car. Once I go inside the store I am heavily burdened and majorly in charge. In this car I'm a background extra, a safe witness. My phone rings, sounding extra loud in the quiet moment I've created with my stalling. Anita.

"Hello?"

"Are you at the store? It's three til nine and you know New-Girl-Jenny is coming today and if you're not at the store I'm going to feel like I can never leave again and I don't want to feel that way, Leona!"

There's a bunch of tooting and crinkling in the background. It sounds like warbling birds, if the birds have swallowed packing peanuts and poker chips.

I open the car door. "I'm just about to walk in. Everything's fine." I don't tell her about the bracelet, but I think of it now as evidence of the fine-ness I've claimed.

"Okay. You're there. I feel better. You'll be fine. I've left lists. You know what to do. I trust you, Leona."

"Thank you." I put the key in the lock. Anita had handed it to me two days ago and said, "It's not that I trust you, Leona. It's that you're my best option."

The door opens and the place smells sweet, like carpet that's been splashed with soda many, many times. I say to my phone, "I'm in" and realize Anita's already hung up. She's out.

I let the door close behind me, and I point authoritatively toward the cash register, then the security camera, then the single dressing room, then at the thirst trap corner. It's all there, and I know it. Point point point, easy. Parameters claimed and doable.

* * *

New-Girl-Jenny shows up with a ponytail that feels defiantly juvenile, and I'm immediately worried about being a person who's trying to tell her what to do. Society and culture have told her that adult women don't do that to their hair, and yet here she is starting a job with a side-pony you can't even call a side-pony because it's behind the ear—a no-man's-land pony. A Droopy-Dog's-left-ear pony. As I tell her my name and point to where she can put her purse, I decide it would be more troubling if she had replicated this same pony on the other side of her head. Maybe part of her knows it's a ridiculous look and stopped her from forming symmetry around it.

Jenny glances at our rows, stacks, and bins. She lets me do all the talking, which makes me feel like I'm trying to sell *her* on this job, on this business, on my own decision to work here. I resent having to justify the existence of our used Halloween costume rack. It looks like we skin superheroes.

I hand her the stack of paperwork. "Anita needs you to fill these out. Sign everything."

Jenny nods at the tax form like she's met it before then asks me, "So what's Anita's deal?"

"What do you mean?"

"I mean, like, does she suck or does she not suck?" She sticks the tip of her tongue over one of her front teeth, like that somehow clarifies the question.

"Anita won't be back until Saturday."

"But, like, as a *boss*? Does she suck to work for?"

What is she suggesting by asking me this? That we are somehow coconspirators? I'm no New-Girl-Jenny cohort. I'm no tittering snitch. Listen, Jenny-Jenny, it's not me and you against Anita. I'm on Anita's level, nearly, and she and I will teach and assess *you*. We have folding techniques to impart. I consider scoffing and pointing at her hair, but then I remember this post I saw and liked just this morning, right after the fucking ocean trash event popped up. It was about supporting other women. The post was actually two animated llamas in skirts trying to square dance and stepping all over each other, but the caption was: "Get it together lladies."

With this animated-yet-applicable sentiment in mind, I tell her, "Anita is a fair and energetic boss. She's very sure about how things should be done, which is a comfort to her employees."

Jenny laughs and says I'm "so funny," which makes me think she may have seen the llady llamas this morning too. Look at us, two feminists, avoiding each other's toes.

* * *

I show Jenny the pricing formulas and buy-back protocols and corduroy slack stacks. She seems to be taking it all in neutrally, which I appreciate after her overly familiar and pointed question about Anita. She's nodding a lot, so she's getting it, but the nodding engages and emphasizes her ponytail, which undermines the obedience and seriousness of her nodding. It's like teaching a bloodhound to distinguish traffic signage—his eye contact might suggest he's learning, but when his tongue falls out during the lesson you both feel silly about wasting your time.

I show her the "husky" section, which is slowly overtaking the store. It's my understanding that kids cannot go outside for exercise nor play because danger lurks, so they stay inside and play video games or watch movies so they can be the perpetrators of violence and chaos, or the consumers of violence and chaos, instead of the victims of violence and chaos. Parents (understandably) don't want anything to *happen* to their kids. They want their kids to happen to life, to make an indoor impact that reverberates through all other indoor spaces via the internet, so that the parents' high school classmates can sit right on their own couches and see how well all the kids are turning out—how, for instance, they wrote the best essay on not letting food waste ruin your appetite—and the classmates (plus the aunts, plus the former coworkers) "like" the kids' accomplishment, and then all of their lives are a complete, meaningful circuit.

I actually say most of this out loud to Jenny, but she doesn't nod at this part. She says, "Oh my god. That's the saddest thing I've ever heard."

I'm pulling down outfits to show her. There's a red jumpsuit that actually used to be a cover for an oval doggie bed, to which some crafty mother added a fashionable collar. "Which part's sad? Food waste ruining your meal?"

Jenny opens her mouth but seems to be unable to decide what to say next. She's learned a lot today, so much new information. She finally says, "I have no idea if you're joking or not. I thought you were before, but now I'm not sure."

Oh god, did I accidentally say "thirst trap" when I was showing her all the corners?

"It's like you see things so clearly, but at the same time you reach the wrong conclusions about what you see."

"You mean you don't like the dog-bed jumpsuit?" I point out the stitching around the collar.

Jenny's mouth opens again while she looks from the jumpsuit to my face over and over. She finally says, "I like it just fine."

* * *

By the time our other day employee, Desiree, shows up, I feel like Jenny knows enough to do a heavily supervised shift. There's no way I can convey to her *all* that I know about the inner-workings of Infant Replay in only a couple hours. I haven't listed all the hashtags from the relevant EffPep post for her yet. I haven't even shown her the blue-liquid spray bottle we use to sanitize the used toys.

I introduce Desiree to Jenny. Desiree says, "Hey." Then, "You always wear your hair like that?" Desiree does not do social media, and in addition to not having access to the right mood-correcting drawings, she might be sour about Anita choosing me to run the store because she technically has seniority. I look at Jenny. Will she fire back? I've never seen firing back in real life, only online. What if I have to make Desiree and Jenny sit in a circle and process their pain and navigate toward common ground and issue public apology videos to each other?

But no, Jenny laughs at Desiree's question. I guess this shouldn't surprise me—Jenny's spent the last two hours finding everything other than written numbers and polyester blends either funny or sad. She's like that two-headed keychain my high school drama teacher had attached to her Volvo fob. Jenny touches her hair and says, "My daughter made me this ponytail for good luck. I meant to take it out before I got here."

"Oh good. I thought you were crazy. Didn't you think she was crazy, Leona, coming in here like that?" Desiree looks at me like I should be able to easily answer this question.

Jenny has pulled out the hair tie and is trying to flatten that piece of hair back down. We open in five minutes. I say, "Sure I noticed. It's part of her head."

* * *

Once we are open, the day moves swiftly. The good thing about working resale is that the giving of money balances out the taking, so you're not like those straight-retail slobs, peddling all incarnations of plastic products. There's a feeling of warm mercy in handing someone thirteen dollars in exchange for six pairs of overalls they have absolutely no use for.

Jenny keeps up, she stays close, except for when I send her out to perform specific tasks, like, "Go hang these dresses over in formal wear, Jenny. This time of year there're always a lot of last-minute funerals, and parents want dark velvets to make it look like the kids will miss their great uncles."

I'm finding Jenny to be pleasant to work with. She's a quick learner, friendly with the customers, and the small section of her hair that refuses to lie down reminds me of the good times we spent together this morning talking about how life is *so funny* and yet *so sad*.

I plan on reporting to Anita that Jenny is a keeper and that Desiree was wholly adequate in her role as "wrangler." We all take turns being the wrangler—the one who deals with the customers' children. The job involves picking fallen tots up out of soda puddles by their belt loops, reuniting kids who hid inside of circular clothing racks with the parents who are only partially relieved to see them again, and standing between slapping siblings to act as a buffer while their mother decides between shoes that fit now but barely and shoes that will fit next month but in the meantime will flop about the heel.

Desiree leaves at 4:00 and becomes whoever she is outside of her employment parameters. Maybe she bakes and plays the mandolin and hardly ever sits numb on her tile. She's replaced by Tyler, our high school employee who works from after school until closing. I don't know his backstory because I respect the boundary he's created with his silence. I secretly imagine that the reason this male teen has chosen to work at a used kids clothing store is because he is the youngest of four brothers, and he never got to pick out his own outfits. He had no choice but to wear hand-me-downs, which had pockets and stripes and corporate grins in places that felt unauthentic to his true nature. He works here to be close to all the choices he didn't get to make.

The three of us deftly handle the after-work crowd, which is composed of parents who've had trash bags of clothes in their trunk for weeks and are finally off-loading them, or parents who've forgotten an important clothing deadline like "red cloak for school play" or "dress shoes for wedding photos" or, most often, "shorts for sports." I put Jenny on wrangling duty, which is a big ask for her first day, but I feel she's up for it. Tyler joins me behind the counter. As I work the register, I keep an eye on Jenny, watching as she puts too-high children (the climbers) back down and too-low children (the fallers and wallowers) back up. She does all this tot-righting with a calm-faced spunk I find contagious. I'm so buoyed that I tell a young mother her baby looks like Ginger Rogers—a dancer with a face actually worth galloping about.

When it's time for Jenny and Tyler to leave, he bows out quietly so we don't notice how many sleeves he fondles along the way, while she takes her time collecting her things. I pause my vacuuming and say,

"You did really well today. I noticed that you didn't go to the bathroom and emerge tear-streaked. I think you're a great addition."

Jenny's face is the sad crying part of that keychain trying to be the laughing part. She says, "Well . . . I need the money." Before she opens the door she says, "See you tomorrow, Leona," and I wave and turn the vacuum back on. Right as the machine vrooms up, Jenny starts to say something more, but when I turn off the motor to hear her she's already on the sidewalk outside, walking toward her car and its glass/steel/rubber/plastic parameters.

* * *

At home, I sit on the tiles even though I was so recently competently managing a resale establishment. I consider calling Anita but decide against it. She's probably sprawled on a hotel bed watching Drayden eat carbs out of Styrofoam while she's being comforted by my lack of checking in.

I want to text Jenny and ask what she was going to say before I sucked up her words. I have her number because bosses must be able to contact their employees about shift changes or inclement weather or sudden-onset bowel issues.

I open a message, type "Jenny," and hit send.

She doesn't respond, and I send, "I understand what you mean about how I see things clearly and then reach . . . limited conclusions."

She doesn't respond, and I send, "I worked hard to achieve a narrow focus. I was once concerned about everything! The income gap, police brutality, climate change, fascism, unwanted pets, diet culture, Amazon. com, the narrow confinements of gender, institutional racism, rising anti-intellectualism, YOU KNOW THE LIST."

She doesn't respond, and I send, "I was barely functional when I got this job. I was always late because I'd be sitting on my bed immobilized about the honey bees. But Anita changed my life. She forced me to pick one worry to focus on and let the rest go. I chose our overdependence on plastic—how it never breaks down and never goes away. I'm super zoned in on that. Sure, I still use a lot of plastics, but

I'm very AWARE of my use. Anita allows me to dig through the trash and take the plastic home to my own recycling bin. That's how I've taken control of the swirling overcast."

I read back over what I've sent. It's all what I meant to say. I turn the volume all-up and stare hard at the screen, so there's no way I'll miss what Jenny has to say about how I've conquered my demons to such an extent that I was given keys.

A ringtone blasts so loud that I drop my phone onto my bath mat. Anita is calling. But then, from down on the bath mat, a message notification peeks over the top of my screen, and I see that it's from Jenny before it peeks away. I pick up the phone and end the incoming call. As I navigate toward Jenny's message, I think about how nimbly she lowered the child she caught scaling the mound of winter coats, how she'd worn a sloppy wandering ponytail for her daughter, how we'll see each other tomorrow.

I open her message. "Thanks for this riot. I GET YOU now. Hilarious."

She *gets* me now. I imagine myself through her eyes: charmless bracelet wearer, ponytail ignorer, plastic crusader, Anita defender. I try smiling at this image of myself, to try and get the joke that is me.

I get another message. Anita asks, "How did it go today?"

I type a thumbs up and then, "I can't stop smiling about it."

Acknowledgements

I am thankful for the love of my little family in our little house. Colin's steady heart, Edith's deep thoughts, and Joan's bouncing joy are my favorite things.

I'm thankful for the love of my big family, too: the Woods, the Barrs, the Bassetts, and anyone else who's ever claimed me. Special thanks to Mom and Dad for never, ever being boring.

I wish I could hand this book to my grandparents. They were good friends of mine.

I am grateful for friendship, guidance, and moral support from Amy Stuber, Emily Koehn, Sara Flannery Murphy, Kyla Skyles, Renae Cole, and lil sister Casey Barr—my original friend/original enemy.

Appreciation and thank yous to my Split Lip family and to the St. Louis Regional Arts Commission.

Lastly, a shout-out to all the dogs and cats who stare at me from interior windows as I pace the sidewalks. The look in their eyes reminds me that I'm an idiot but that I mean well.

Source Acknowledgments

American Literary Review: "Prove It"

HAD: "Bulk Trash Is for Lovers"

Hysterical Rag: "Enviable Levels"

Longleaf Review: "Perceptor Weekly"

New Delta Review: "More Restrictive Than Supportive"

No Contact: "No Space Is Too Small When Your Head Is Detachable"

Okay Donkey: "The Right Light"

Superstition Review: "Thanks for This Riot"

Trampset: "All I Need Are These Four Walls
and Some Positive Feedback"

VIDA Review: "These New Francescas"

X-R-A-Y: "Babies Don't Keep"

In the Raz/Shumaker Prairie Schooner Book Prize in Fiction series

To order or obtain more information on these or other University of
Nebraska Press titles, visit nebraskapress.unl.edu.

Printed in the USA
CPSIA information can be obtained
at www.ICGtesting.com
LVHW090243201124
797134LV00002B/173